LILY
TO THE rescue

Books 4–6

Lily to the Rescue: Dog Dog Goose
Lily to the Rescue: Lost Little Leopard
Lily to the Rescue: The Misfit Donkey

W. BRUCE CAMERON

LILY
TO THE rescue

Books 4–6

Lily to the Rescue: Dog Dog Goose
Lily to the Rescue: Lost Little Leopard
Lily to the Rescue: The Misfit Donkey

Illustrations by

JENNIFER L. MEYER

JAMES BERNARDIN

TOR PUBLISHING GROUP

NEW YORK

LILY TO THE RESCUE BIND-UP BOOKS 4–6: DOG DOG GOOSE, LOST LITTLE LEOPARD, AND THE MISFIT DONKEY

Lily to the Rescue: Dog Dog Goose copyright © 2020 by W. Bruce Cameron
Lily to the Rescue: Lost Little Leopard copyright © 2021 by W. Bruce Cameron
Lily to the Rescue: The Misfit Donkey copyright © 2021 by W. Bruce Cameron

Lily to the Rescue: Dog Dog Goose illustrations © 2020 by Jennifer L. Meyer
Lily to the Rescue: Lost Little Leopard illustrations © 2021 by James Bernardin
Lily to the Rescue: The Misfit Donkey illustrations © 2021 by James Bernardin

A Starscape Book
Published by Tom Doherty Associates / Tor Publishing Group
120 Broadway
New York, NY 10271

www.tor-forge.com

ISBN 978-1-250-86766-7 (trade paperback)

Our books may be purchased in bulk for promotional, educational, or business use. Please contact your local bookseller or the Macmillan Corporate and Premium Sales Department at 1-800-221-7945, extension 5442, or by email at MacmillanSpecialMarkets@macmillan.com.

First Edition: 2023

Printed in the United States of America

0 9 8 7 6 5 4 3 2 1

Contents

Lily to the Rescue: Dog Dog Goose   1

Lily to the Rescue: Lost Little Leopard   131

Lily to the Rescue: The Misfit Donkey   247

LILY
TO THE rescue

DOG
DOG GOOSE

Dedicated to the wonderful people helping animals at Wayside Waifs in Kansas City.

I am a dog, and my name is Lily. I have a girl, and her name is Maggie Rose.

Today Maggie Rose put me on a leash. That meant I was going someplace exciting!

I trotted on my leash beside Maggie Rose. Craig walked with us. He is Maggie Rose's much older brother, and from where I stand, he looks very tall. Maggie Rose has another brother named Bryan, but he is not as tall, and he was not walking with us today.

My job when I am walking with Maggie Rose is to look for things that she might not notice, such as a squirrel who needs to be chased, or bushes where dogs have lifted their legs.

"Know what kind of ice cream cone you want, Maggie Rose?" Craig asked while I was busy sniffing one of those bushes.

"Strawberry, because it's pink. Pink's my favorite color," Maggie replied.

"I thought you liked vanilla ice cream with sprinkles on it," Craig objected.

Maggie Rose frowned. "That was last year, when I was in second grade. I'm a third-grader now, so I like strawberry."

Craig nodded. "Makes sense."

A car drove past us on the street. A dog had his head out the window, and he barked at me. I knew what he was trying to tell me: "I'm in the car and you're not! I'm in the car and you're not!"

He kept barking until the car turned a corner. Some dogs are like that. They start barking and then they just don't stop, even if they have forgotten why they were barking in the first place. I am a well-behaved dog, and I do not do such things.

We walked a little more, and then Craig went inside a building while I stayed outside with Maggie Rose. In a little while, Craig was back. He was carrying an ice cream cone in each hand, which I thought was a wonderful thing to do!

They sat at a table, and I did Sit. I am extremely good at Sit. I was sure that when Maggie Rose noticed what an incredible Sit I was doing, I would get some of that ice cream. Nothing else would even make sense.

But then a loud, deep voice startled us all. "Go away!" a man shouted.

We all jumped. I looked over my shoulder. There was a parking lot behind us, and a man was standing at the edge of it, looking angrily into a little stretch of trees and bushes. "Go away!" he shouted again.

"Whoa," Craig said. "It's Mr. Swanson! You know, he lives two houses down." He raised his voice a little. "What's going on, Mr. Swanson?"

Mr. Swanson turned around to look at us. He walked up to our table and pointed one thumb over his shoulder. "Hi, kids. See the fox?"

Craig shook his head. "What fox?" said Maggie Rose.

Mr. Swanson pointed into the trees. "There. Right there. See it?"

We all looked into the woods. I lifted my nose, and I caught a scent that was new to me. It was like a male dog, but different— wilder and more fierce. I pulled on my leash a little, so that Maggie Rose would let me go and meet this new animal. We could play together!

I am very good at playing with other animals. I often go to a place called Work and play with all the animals there. Work is where Mom spends most of her time helping animals. She calls Work "the rescue."

Maggie Rose twitched. "I see it! Lily, do you see it? See the fox?"

That was a new word to me—"fox." It must be the name of the animal.

The fox was crouched behind a bush, so I could only catch a glimpse of short fur and bright eyes and ears that stood up in stiff triangles. He stared at us hard.

"He's here for the eggs," Mr. Swanson said.

"What eggs?" Maggie Rose asked.

"Come on, I'll show you."

Mr. Swanson took us toward a big wooden box in the middle of the parking lot. It had some bushes and flowers growing inside it.

"A goose laid some eggs right in this planter," Mr. Swanson said. "But a couple of days ago, some men were here fixing potholes in the parking lot, and I guess the noise scared her. She flew away and never came back."

"Oh no," said Maggie Rose.

When we reached the wooden box, Maggie Rose looked into it. She gasped.

Craig peered over her shoulder. "Whoa, look at that!"

"Well, now," Mr. Swanson said. "That's remarkable!"

I put my front feet on the edge of the wooden box so that I could see inside. There was something moving in there!

Actually, there were a lot of somethings. They were small and fuzzy, like the kittens I play with at Work sometimes. But they also had beaks, like my friend Casey the crow. (Casey spent some time at Work because Mom needed to help his wing, so we got to know each other really well.) They huddled together in a group making tiny peeping noises. Broken eggshells were all around them.

"The eggs hatched!" exclaimed Maggie Rose. "They're so cute!"

"They're cute, all right," Craig said. He didn't sound as happy as Maggie Rose did. "But where's their mom?"

"Hasn't been back since she flew off," Mr. Swanson said, shaking his head.

"Let's put Lily in the planter with the baby geese," Maggie Rose suggested. "She will protect them from the fox."

At the word "fox" I turned to smell for the animal in the woods, but it had run off without even trying to be friends. I thought that was very unfriendly. Life would be better if all animals acted more like dogs.

Maggie Rose picked me up. "They must be scared without their mom."

"They're going to be even more scared if a dog's in there with them," Mr. Swanson warned her.

"Actually, my sister might be right," Craig answered.

"Lily helps out at the rescue all the time,"

Maggie Rose explained to Mr. Swanson. "She plays with all the animals."

"If you say so," Mr. Swanson replied doubtfully.

Maggie Rose put me inside the big wooden box. "Be nice to the baby geese, Lily," she told me.

2

I stood still and waited. I have learned that new animals don't always like it if I rush at them and sniff their butts, which is the polite way to get to know one another for dogs. Sometimes they need time to understand that I just want to play.

Not these little creatures, though. They rushed toward me. It was funny! They didn't pounce like kittens, and they didn't fly like grownup birds, and they didn't run like

puppies. They moved in their own way, with a waddle.

I put my nose down to sniff them. They smelled very interesting—fluffy and feathery and young. They clustered around my muzzle and nibbled on my whiskers with their tiny beaks. It didn't hurt. They were too small to hurt anybody. They really seemed to like me!

"Well, would you look at that," Mr. Swanson

said. "It's like they understand why you put your dog in there with them!"

"It's kind of amazing," Craig agreed. "I've seen Lily play with kittens and grumpy old dogs and a ferret and even a crow."

"So now she's friends with the baby geese!" my girl exclaimed happily.

"Goslings," Craig replied.

"Huh?"

"Baby geese are called goslings."

"Goslings," Maggie Rose repeated. "Goslings."

I heard that word, goslings. I decided the tiny birds were goslings. That's why Maggie Rose and Craig kept saying it.

"Don't know what to feed them," Mr. Swanson said. "I could bring some water, I guess. But I don't know where to get goose milk."

Craig laughed. Maggie Rose smiled a little.

"They're birds, not mammals, Mr. Swanson," she explained. "They don't drink milk."

"Oh, right," Mr. Swanson said. "I wasn't thinking straight. Fact is, I was thinking about my wife."

"About Mrs. Swanson?" Maggie Rose asked.

Mr. Swanson nodded. "She's goose-crazy, to tell you the truth. Anything with a picture of a goose on it, she'll buy it. She's got a collection of goose eggs. She'd have geese of her own if she could, but I'm allergic to their feathers. Can't even wear a down jacket. I wondered for a while if she'd pick geese over me, but so far she's stuck with me. But I bet she won't if she finds out I let anything happen to these little fellas."

"That fox will get them for sure if the mom doesn't come back," Craig said. "We better ask Mom and Dad what to do."

Mr. Swanson nodded. "That's right, I forgot—your mother runs that animal rescue." He dug in his back pocket. "Here, use my phone."

Craig took the phone. Human beings seem to like phones a lot. They stare at them and touch them and talk to them all the time, even with a dog in the room. I do not know why. Phones do not smell at all interesting.

"Good dog," Maggie Rose said. She took a bite of her ice cream. I stared at it unhappily—it was almost gone!

Craig had stopped talking to the phone. "Mom'll be here in a minute," he said. His ice cream *was* gone!

So apparently it was the part of the day where a good dog who wasn't getting any ice cream was supposed to stay in a box with a bunch of baby birds called goslings. I nudged a few of them aside and lay down and at once they were huddled all around me, trying to cuddle right up to my nose. I was worried that if I yawned they might try to climb into my mouth!

"Good, gentle girl," Maggie Rose praised. I heard a car pull up near us in the parking lot, and moments later I smelled Mom standing next to my girl. I wagged my tail very gently, so Mom would know I was glad to see her but I wouldn't knock any baby birds out of the box.

"Oh boy," Mom said, looking down at me.

"What's wrong, Mom?" Craig asked.

"Lily's protecting the goslings," my girl said proudly.

"I see that. And that's probably going to be a problem."

"Why?"

"Mr. Swanson," Mom asked, "when was the last time you saw the mother goose?"

"At least two days ago," Mr. Swanson said.

Mom shook her head. "Two days? That's too long. If the mom was going to come back, she'd have been here by now. And no sign of the father at all?"

"Never seen more than one goose by the nest," Mr. Swanson said.

"Well, the father would have been nearby, but you might not have seen him. He'd be keeping an eye on the nest, but out of sight, so he wouldn't attract predators."

"So they're not coming back?" Maggie Rose asked.

"Probably not," Mom said.

"Why did you say there's a problem, Mom?" Craig pressed.

"See, geese are imprinting birds," Mom said.

"Printing?" Mr. Swanson repeated, puzzled.

"Not printing. *Im*printing."

Maggie Rose's forehead wrinkled. "What does that mean?"

"When goslings hatch, they can't do much of anything for themselves," Mom explained. "So the very first thing they do is look around for their mother. Usually she's right there, sitting on the nest. But if she's gone for some reason, then the babies will decide that whatever animal they see first must be their mom. They'll follow that animal everywhere, and learn how to behave from it."

"Uh-oh," Maggie Rose said.

"There's no way either of you could have

known. Lily has been so good at helping our rescued animals feel welcome and safe. So naturally, you put her in the planter to calm the goslings. You didn't know about imprinting.

"It's unusual for geese to imprint on a dog, but it's happened," Mom continued. "And there's no way that I know of to change it."

"So the babies think Lily is their mother?" my girl asked. "And they think Lily's going to teach them how to be geese?"

Mom nodded. "Yes, exactly."

3

Mom pulled a small crate out of the back of the car. Then she reached for a handful of goslings. They were frightened, and they peeped and tried to dart away. I didn't move—I've learned that when animals are scared, it helps for me to lie still.

"Quick, everybody!" Mom urged.

Craig and Mr. Swanson both reached in to pick up goslings. "They're so light!" Craig said. "It's like holding air!"

Mr. Swanson managed to snag only one. "They're quick little things!" he said.

Maggie Rose didn't try to pick up any of the goslings. Instead, she picked *me* up.

"Take care of them, Lily," she said, and she put me inside the crate, too. The crate with the birds and me went into the car.

I have been in lots of crates. The first time I didn't like it, because it kept me apart from Maggie Rose. But I have learned not to mind. My girl always lets me out again in time, and meanwhile it is cozy to curl up and have a nap.

That's what I did. As the car started moving, I carefully checked to make sure there were no goslings beneath me, and lay down.

Peep! A high-pitched noise came from under my belly. I looked down in surprise to see a fuzzy little gosling wiggling out from underneath me. I must have missed one!

I gave it a lick and it wiggled its head and peeped some more.

We drove a little way, and then we stopped at Work.

I love Work!

Work is where so many of my friends live. There is Brewster the old dog, and sometimes Freddy the ferret comes to visit, and lots of cats and kittens and now and then a squirrel. We even had a couple of baby pigs once! There is always someone to play with at Work, though this would be the first time we had a whole flock of baby birds.

Mom carried the crate with the goslings and me inside the building. They seemed scared at the way the crate floor tilted and swung, staring at me as if expecting me to do something about it. All they did was peep, though—the same noise they'd been making the whole time.

Mom set my crate down in a larger pen, the kind that is called a kennel. Maggie Rose came inside the kennel, too.

Mom opened up the crate. The goslings stayed inside, huddled close to me, peeping.

"Call Lily," Mom said softly to Maggie Rose. "I bet if she comes out, the goslings will, too."

My girl called my name, and I went to her because I am a good dog. The goslings followed me out of the crate. They looked around the kennel and peeped in confusion.

"Okay," Mom said. She reached over to rub my ears and I leaned into it, groaning a little. "You can let Lily out of the kennel. I'll go get some goose food."

Mom left the room and Maggie Rose slipped me out of the kennel and closed the gate. I heard the goslings peeping very loudly behind me.

I wandered over to Brewster's kennel and whined at Maggie Rose until she let me in.

Brewster was curled up on his blanket in a corner. He lifted his head when I trotted in and sniffed him. Brewster is a friend of mine, even though he does not like to spend much time playing Chase-Me or I've-Got-the-Ball or Tug-on-a-Stick. He is old and prefers napping over playing.

Brewster smelled like food, and like the blanket he lay on, and like himself. He also smelled a lot like Bryan.

Bryan did not come to get ice cream with us. Brewster's fur smelled like Bryan most days. That was funny, because Brewster lived at Work and Bryan lived at Home. Why

would Bryan's scent be on Brewster? Were they napping together?

By now the goslings were making so much noise that Brewster groaned. He gave me a look as if this were somehow all my fault, which was ridiculous.

"Lily! Lily, come!" Maggie Rose was kneeling next to the kennel with the goslings inside.

I hurried away from Brewster. When I reached my girl, the goslings rushed over to strain against the wire of the kennel,

sticking their beaks out and peeping at me with their tiny voices.

Mom came back in the room, carrying a box. "I could hear them all the way from the supply kitchen," she remarked.

"They seem really upset that Lily is out and they're not. But I knew you would want them to stay in the kennel; they were so hard to catch the first time."

"Oh, I think they'll stick right by your dog no matter what," Mom replied.

I wagged at the word "dog."

"Open the kennel," Mom suggested.

Maggie Rose reached over to the kennel door and opened it up.

"Come on out, baby geese," she said.

The baby birds poured out of the kennel and frantically rushed over to me as if they hadn't been able to see I was right there the whole time. They tried to climb up onto me and fell off onto the floor and peeped and struggled to their feet again for another try. My girl stood up so they wouldn't try to climb on her, which was only right—I am Maggie Rose's dog, and if anyone was going to climb up on her, it should be me.

"Good dog, Lily," she told me.

I didn't even look up, because I'd been called "good dog" a lot lately, but before there had been no ice cream and I could smell there were no treats now.

Mom put the box that she was carrying down onto the floor and I went to examine it, the geese right on my heels. Inside it were seeds and pieces of grass and some small berries. Why bother to put stuff like that in a box?

The goslings seemed to be very interested in the box, though. Its sides were very low and they could climb right into it. They began waddling among the grass and seeds and berries, pecking and nibbling and peeping.

The things in that box were bird treats, then? I did not understand this at all. I'd done Come and Sit for Maggie Rose, but the little geese had not done anything except peep and climb all over me like I was a bird bed.

I padded over to a bowl of water and drank. Then, with a long, weary sigh, I flopped down on the floor and stretched out on my side for a nap like old Brewster.

Peep peep peep! Goslings instantly rushed over to surround me.

It seemed that these geese wanted to be really, really good friends with me! They nestled around me, huddling into my fur, pecking lightly at my skin.

"I think Lily will have to stay the night," Mom said. "The goslings won't be able to settle down without her."

"Can I stay, too?" Maggie Rose asked. "I can sleep on the couch."

Mom shook her head. "No, because Lily will want to lie with you, and the goslings will want to lie with her, and you'll end up sleeping with baby geese. You might roll over and crush them. Nope, I'm afraid Lily is going to have to handle her job as the new mother goose all by herself."

My girl's shoulders slumped. "I am going to miss my dog."

"I'm sure she'll miss you, too," Mom replied, "but if we separate her from them, it might make the goslings really, really upset."

There was some more talking, and after a while Maggie Rose brought me a whole bowl of food all for myself. I had to shake goslings off to eat it, and they peeped at me until I lay back down so they could snuggle beside me again.

This was getting to be ridiculous. I was

very much looking forward to going Home so I could sleep with my girl.

Except *that's not what happened*. Maggie Rose put me inside the goslings' kennel and left me there and went away!

I barked a little to remind her that she had forgotten me, but she didn't come back. I whined a few times, but that didn't work, either. Meanwhile the baby birds stared up at me as if I was waving an ice cream cone around. *What did they want?*

Brewster groaned and got up and circled around and lay back down, and as he did so he gave me a weary look, probably thinking I looked very silly with a bunch of goslings clinging to me.

Slowly the room got darker, although a little light still came in through a window. I sighed. A few goslings peeped. Then everything was quiet for a while, until something went *click*.

It was a door. The door was opening.

Someone came through the door, someone who smelled familiar. It was Bryan.

Bryan came into the room where I was in the kennel with the goslings. He was carrying the long stick that he sometimes uses to hit balls. He put the stick and a ball and a

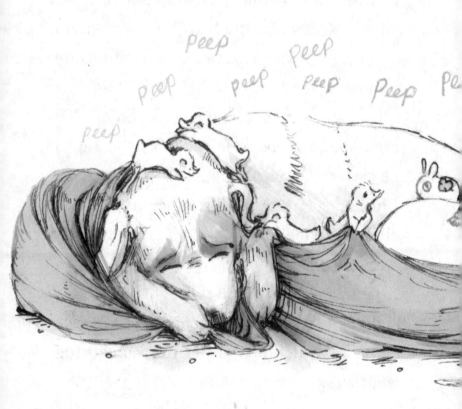

big leather glove down by the wall. Then he came over to my kennel.

He unlatched the door and looked in. "Lily, is that you?" he asked. "What are you doing with all those ducks?" He opened my kennel door.

I wagged my tail but didn't get up because I had all these peeping geese sticking to me. Bryan shrugged and kept moving. He stopped in front of Brewster's kennel.

"Hi, boy," I heard him say.

ep

peep

Bryan opened up the kennel door and Brewster actually climbed to his feet. Bryan pulled some treats out of his pocket and gave them to Brewster.

Okay, I was a good dog, too, just like Brewster. I got up, shaking off goslings, and left the kennel to go over to Bryan and Brewster.

The goslings followed me,

of course. They probably thought they were dogs, but that was just silly. Dogs know how to do Sit and Stay and Lie Down and Roll Over, and that is why they get treats. Other animals don't do these things, and that's why treats are not for them.

Well, every now and then cats get treats. But they don't really deserve them.

Bryan understood. He gave me a treat and did not give any to the goslings. I loved Bryan. Also, his hands smelled a little like peanut butter, and I love peanut butter.

Bryan sat down on the floor and leaned his back up against one wall of the kennel. Brewster lay down next to him and put his head in Bryan's lap. Bryan rubbed his ears and stroked his head, and Brewster let out a long groan of happiness.

"You're a good dog," Bryan whispered. "A good, good dog."

They stayed like that for a while. I did Sit

in case Bryan had any more treats hidden in his pockets. The goslings clustered around my feet and settled down. Brewster looked away, embarrassed for me.

After a while, Bryan sighed. "I have to go now," he said. Very gently, he picked up Brewster's head and put it on the ground. "Sorry, boy. I'll be back."

Then with a loud noise we heard the side door open. "Lily!"

It was my girl! She came rushing into the room of kennels and halted in surprise when she saw her brother in the kennel with Brewster's head in his lap.

"Bryan?" she said.

"Don't tell Mom," he whispered urgently.

5

I was greeting Maggie Rose with licks and wags while the goslings milled around underfoot, as if they didn't understand how wonderful it was that my girl had come back.

"What are you doing here, Bryan?" Maggie Rose asked.

"Maggie Rose, are you talking to me?" Mom called from another room at Work.

"Um . . . I am here with Lily!" my girl called back.

I wagged at my name.

Bryan stood up. Brewster did Sit at his feet.

"I'm just visiting Brewster," Bryan explained quietly.

"But it's after dinner," Maggie Rose said.

"So what? I can't pet a dog after dinner?"

"You told Mom and Dad you were playing baseball with your friends!"

"Yeah, well." Bryan looked embarrassed.

I lay down and rolled over, and the baby birds scattered when my girl started rubbing my tummy.

"You play baseball with your friends every night!" Maggie Rose went on.

"No, I don't," Bryan said. "I come to visit Brewster after dinner every night."

"You do?" Maggie Rose stopped rubbing my tummy. She straightened up and the goslings all rushed to be with me even though I had been lying here the whole time. I wearily got to my feet and did Sit like Brewster.

"He's all by himself. All night long," Bryan said. "I just . . . visit him. That's all. Don't tell anybody, Maggie Rose!"

My girl's eyes widened. "You should adopt Brewster!" she said.

Bryan made a snorting kind of noise. I looked at him in surprise. Humans don't usually snort.

"Mom would never let me," he said. "You know her and her rules—our family can't adopt animals from the Rescue because it sets a bad example, somehow."

"They let me have Lily," Maggie Rose pointed out.

"That's different. That's because you're the youngest," Bryan said. "And they love Craig because he's the oldest and responsible and stuff. But they're not going to let *me* have a dog. There's no point even asking."

"Except Brewster is a senior dog. Mom says it is really hard to place an old dog with a new family," Lily argued.

Brewster and I both wagged at "dog" but the goslings didn't react at all. They were still staring at me as if I were a human with bird treats in my pocket.

Bryan didn't say anything. The goslings poked their beaks into my fur.

"What if you paid the adoption fee?" Maggie Rose suggested suddenly.

Bryan snorted again. Brewster and I glanced at each other. I wondered if Bryan was going to be making this noise all the time now.

"I don't have anywhere near that much money," he replied. "It's, like, two hundred dollars."

"But if you did," Maggie Rose insisted, "I'll bet you Mom would say yes."

"Whatever. It's way more than I have."

"But I have money, too," Maggie Rose pointed out.

Bryan stared at her. Brewster flopped down on the floor with a groan. I didn't, because if I did I would be swarmed with goslings.

"I'll give you all my money," Maggie Rose continued. "And then we can do extra chores around the house to earn more. If you had the adoption fee, Mom would have to say yes!"

"You would do that for me?"

"For you and for Brewster."

Brewster had been snoozing, but he opened a lazy eye when my girl said his name.

"Okay!" Bryan replied.

"Maggie Rose?" called a voice from the door to the yard. "I'm done closing up for the night—time to go home. Say bye to Lily."

It was Mom's voice. Bryan made a face at Maggie Rose and held a finger in front of his lips. Maggie Rose nodded at him. He turned to leave through the front door.

"Bryan?" my girl said softly.

Bryan turned back.

"Mom and Dad do love you," Maggie Rose proclaimed. "And so do I."

Bryan snorted. *Again.*

I don't think I understood that my girl was going to leave me at Work so the baby birds could all try to climb on my head, and do it the next day, and the next, and the next.

Had I been a bad dog? Why wasn't I sleeping on my girl's bed?

The geese were with me constantly. They trailed along the floor behind me. They nibbled on my fur and wiggled under my belly. They nestled up close to me as soon as I stopped moving.

Why couldn't they climb on Brewster instead? All he did was lie there. He would make an excellent bird's nest! But no, the goslings wanted to be with just me.

One morning my girl took me and the goslings out into the yard. I went through the dog door by myself, but Maggie Rose had to hold the people door open for the geese.

The yard at Work is a nice place, with grass and one tree with a squirrel who comes down to be chased every now and then. Today the squirrel was not around, though. Instead Craig was there, picking up some papers that had blown into the yard.

"Hey, they've gotten a little bigger already," Craig said.

I wanted to play Chase-Me or Fetch with Craig and Maggie Rose, but it was hard with the geese underfoot. The only game they seemed to know was Follow-Lily-Everywhere.

After a little while, Mom came into the yard with another lady who had been eating bacon for breakfast, which I appreciated very much.

"Oh, they are precious!" the new woman exclaimed, clapping her hands.

I thought maybe she wanted me to come and sniff her. Sometimes people who clap their hands want that. But she wasn't even looking at me. She was looking at the goslings.

"Hi, Mrs. Swanson," Maggie Rose said.

The new lady, I figured out, was called Mrs. Swanson. She liked to talk.

"I just love geese," she said to Mom and Maggie Rose and sort of to me and the goslings, too. "I always have. You know the way some people just love cats? I feel that way about geese. When my husband told me about these poor orphaned babies, I knew I had to come and see them."

The goslings were pecking at my feet. I turned around and nudged them out of the way with my nose so I could go and sniff Mrs. Swanson's shoes.

"Maybe I could help support them?" Mrs. Swanson asked Mom. "I'd love to help buy food for them."

Mom smiled. "We're always looking for donations to support our work," she said.

Mrs. Swanson talked some more and some more and then she and Mom went away. Maggie Rose grinned at me. "She's a little funny," she whispered. "Why would anybody like geese better than dogs, Lily?"

I crawled into her lap. The geese circled around, working up the nerve to climb up with me. Goslings do not always understand that sometimes a dog just wants to be with her girl.

Craig came over to see me but probably not the goslings. "Hey, good dog, Lily," he said, leaning in to talk to my girl.

"So," he murmured quietly. "I know something is going on, Maggie Rose."

 I looked at my girl with interest—she had stiffened, and seemed worried.

"Something going on?" she repeated innocently.

"With you and Bryan. All of a sudden you're doing all these extra jobs around the house? Bryan was sweeping the garage—last time he did that it was because Dad was using it as *punishment*. I saw you straightening the shelves and dusting them. What gives? Did you two do something really bad?" Craig demanded.

"No-o-o," my girl answered slowly.

"Then what? Why are you two working so hard to impress Mom and Dad?"

"Okay, look Craig, if I tell you, you have to promise not to tell anyone else. Okay?"

Craig folded his arms. "You know what Dad always says—you can't make that promise until you know what it is. Like, what if you and Bryan robbed a bank or something? I'd have to tell."

My girl sighed. I thought about lying down on her feet, but I knew as soon as I did I'd be covered with baby birds. "Okay, I'll tell you."

"Good."

Maggie Rose took a deep breath. "Bryan and I robbed a bank."

"Maggie Rose!" Craig was laughing. "Come on."

"Well . . . you know how Mom always says Brewster is a senior dog that nobody will ever want and it's sad because he is so great but people don't adopt old pets?" My girl's words were coming out of her in a rush. "Well, Bryan does want to adopt Brewster!"

Craig was shaking his head. "You know Mom's policy about that. We can foster rescued animals, but if we adopt one that's foster failure, and it sets a bad example for the other people who foster."

"Yes," my girl said, "but she made an exception for me, because Lily is such a special dog. She'll do the same for Bryan—otherwise, it's not fair!"

"I guess it's not fair," Craig agreed, "but you know Mom. She'll come up with a reason that will make sense so she can be both fair and stick to the rules."

Maggie Rose nodded. "That's why Bryan and I are raising money to pay Brewster's adoption fee. If we have the fee, Mom has to say yes, doesn't she?"

Craig looked thoughtful. "You know, this could work. When you say it's not fair to let you have Lily but not let Bryan have Brewster, she'll probably say 'okay, but only if you pay the adoption fee'—because she knows you don't have that kind of money. How much do you have?"

"Almost half . . . of half," my girl admitted hesitantly.

The goslings were all clustered around my butt, as if they wanted me to sit on them. Which meant I couldn't sit, even though I wanted to!

"Okay, well . . . I've got some money saved up, so you guys can have that, too. But you still have a long way to go," Craig told her.

My girl pumped her fist and said "*Yes!*"—so happy to have a dog like me she nearly jumped.

I wish I could say that I went Home and the goslings stayed at Work that night, but instead I was left at Work with Brewster and the silly birds.

I stayed at Work for days and days. I did most of the things I usually did. I sniffed Brewster and my other friends and said hello to all the people who came to take care of the dogs and cats and squirrels and ferrets and birds and other animals who live there. I was a good dog, but I missed my girl at night and I was tired of being climbed on by geese.

Maggie Rose came to see me every day, though. Often she would let me and the goslings out into the yard. I would sniff and the geese would follow me, sometimes climbing over each other to be close to me. They were right there when I squatted.

I don't mind peeing in front of other dogs. But for some reason it is embarrassing to do it in front of baby geese.

Dad had set up a small plastic pool in the yard, and he was standing there filling it up with a hose. I went over and slurped up a drink. Water from a hose tastes different from water in a bowl.

The goslings followed, of course. I was willing to teach them to drink from the hose, but they weren't interested in that. They were focused on the water in the pool.

Dad put a long, flat piece of wood on the ground. One end of the wood was on the edge of the pool and the other was in the grass, so it made a ramp.

"Help them out, Maggie Rose," he said.

Maggie Rose knelt down. "Go on, Gertrude," she said, pushing a gosling up the ramp.

Dad chuckled. "Gertrude?"

"That's her name. She's the biggest,"

Maggie Rose said. "And she's the bravest, too. She does things first, and the rest follow. Okay, Mr. Waddle-puss. Fluffy. Goofy. Downy. Oh, and Harold. You go, too."

She shooed the goslings up the ramp.

When Gertrude reached the top of the ramp, she didn't hesitate. She plunged straight into the water. The other goslings followed her.

I know about water. It's good for drinking when it's in bowls or hoses, but if you try to stand on it or run on it, you go down to the bottom.

But for some reason this water was different! The goslings did not sink. They stayed right on the top, and when they paddled with their legs they moved over the water.

I put my feet up on the edge of the pool to watch this amazing sight. Gertrude paddled right over to me. The others followed. They peeped at me as if they wanted me to get in and swim, but swimming is for geese and not for dogs like me.

Some of them even ducked their bodies under the water. I whined and looked at Maggie Rose. But it turned out that I didn't need to worry. The goslings popped right back up.

"They know how to swim!" Maggie Rose exclaimed.

"Geese can swim at one day old," Dad said.

After that, the goslings swam in the pool every day. And every night I slept in the kennel with a bunch of geese burrowing into me. Brewster kept regarding them sourly, probably thinking I was a poor excuse for a dog with all these birds sitting on me.

Even worse than my embarrassment over being covered with geese was the fact that I was not with Maggie Rose. I missed my girl so much that I finally realized what I had to do:

I needed to escape from Work.

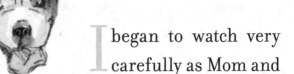

I began to watch very carefully as Mom and my girl left Work every day. They always went out the back door into the yard, which was at the end of a hall. There was a door to that hall, but they only shut it when they were leading dogs to the kennels. Otherwise, it was open. Which meant I could run down the hall and out the dog door. And then Mom always held the gate open for Maggie Rose.

When that gate was open, I would have my chance!

I almost felt like a bad dog, just thinking about bursting through that gate, but I was tired of always being covered in geese, and I belonged with my girl.

One day Craig came to watch the goslings swim. I poked at his leg with my nose to remind him that dogs are important, too. He scratched my ears. Bryan was using a loud machine to blow leaves around in the front yard, and Mrs. Swanson came out to be with us, though she still seemed more interested in the geese than in a good dog who could do Sit and Roll Over.

"I have a lot of fall eggs that I've collected over the years," Mrs. Swanson said to Maggie Rose and Craig. "Would you like to see them?"

Craig looked at Maggie Rose. Maggie Rose

nodded and got my leash and led me to the gate. We slipped out, shutting the geese into the yard. Then we all went on a walk, Maggie Rose and me and Mom and Craig and Mrs. Swanson, too. It felt so good not to have a bunch of birds stepping all over my feet!

We crossed the field and passed Home and walked down the street to a house I'd never been in. It smelled like Mr. and Mrs. Swanson.

We went into the garage. "I'm sorry, it's a little cluttered," Mrs. Swanson said. "I keep meaning to organize it."

"So many geese!" Maggie Rose said. She held my leash and turned from side to side.

"Geese Christmas ornaments. Geese plates," Craig said, looking around.

"Stuffed geese!" Maggie Rose said, pointing.

"Geese statues!" Craig said, pointing somewhere else.

"Kids! Don't be rude," Mom said sternly.

Mrs. Swanson laughed. "They're not

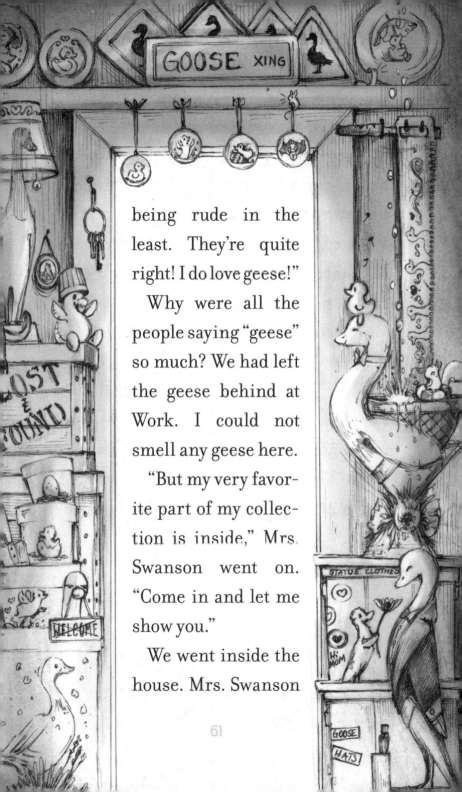

being rude in the least. They're quite right! I do love geese!"

Why were all the people saying "geese" so much? We had left the geese behind at Work. I could not smell any geese here.

"But my very favorite part of my collection is inside," Mrs. Swanson went on. "Come in and let me show you."

We went inside the house. Mrs. Swanson

led us over to a shelf high up on the wall. A row of eggs was lined up on it.

I know about eggs because Mom or Dad cracks them for breakfast, and if there are leftovers they sometimes end up in my bowl. I looked up at these eggs hopefully, but no one seemed to be thinking of a good dog in that moment.

"These are very rare," Mrs. Swanson explained.

"Why?" Craig asked. "Don't geese lay eggs all the time?"

"They aren't ordinary eggs," Mrs. Swanson said. "They're fall eggs. Most geese don't lay eggs until they're a year old, in the spring.

But every now and then a young goose will lay an egg in the fall, right before she migrates. The eggs don't hatch. But sometimes people have one for sale and I'll buy it. They're rare and they're special—the first eggs from a goose!"

They all looked at the eggs for a while and talked some more. I sat down and scratched one of my ears. Then the other one.

At last the people were done talking about geese. Mom and Craig and Maggie Rose and I left.

"I didn't want to ask Mrs. Swanson," Craig said, "but she's had those eggs for years, right? Why don't they stink?"

"If an egg never cracks, it won't stink," Mom said. "The water inside evaporates eventually, and the solid parts of the egg just stay there, dried up, forever."

"Goose mummies," Craig said. "Creepy!"

Maggie Rose squealed and Mom laughed

a little. "That's pretty much right," she said. "That's exactly what fall eggs are!"

"What's 'migrate,' Mom?" my girl asked.

"It's when they fly south for the winter," Craig volunteered.

Mom nodded. "Exactly right. Geese fly out to where it is warm to fatten up, and come back here in the spring. Except our little goslings think that a dog is their mommy. Who is going to teach them to fly? And how will they know where to go if they think they are supposed to spend the winter with a dog?"

Back home the goslings were so overjoyed at my return I had to just stand there and let them flap at me and climb up and prod me with their beaks. Later, I was not able to follow my girl and Mom out the back gate because Maggie Rose fed Brewster and me and my face was in the bowl, frantically licking up every scrap, and then I bolted for the dog door but Mom was already shutting the gate.

So I was just lying there at night, covered in birds, Gertrude huddled closest, Bryan

sitting with Brewster's head in his lap, when I heard a door open.

I lifted my head and sniffed. It was not Maggie Rose coming. It was Dad.

"Bryan?" he called.

Brewster and I both lifted our heads, startled, when Bryan made an alarmed-sounding noise. Dad came into the room. He stopped when he saw Bryan and Brewster.

"Bryan?" Dad said again.

8

Brewster and I could tell something was going on, and the goslings couldn't. Bryan and Dad were both tense. Brewster sat up but I didn't, because if I did the geese would start peeping in confusion and who could put up with that?

"So this is where you've been going every night. I thought you were playing ball with your friends," Dad said. "I went by the park, though, and you weren't there. Maggie Rose told me

I could find
you here."

Bryan muttered something.

It sounded like "not any good."

"What?" Dad asked.

"They won't let me play," Bryan said, staring down at Brewster's head. "I'm not good enough."

Dad frowned. "What do you mean? You do fine with Craig and me."

Bryan shrugged. "I can't hit the ball."

"Well," Dad said. "Let's see about that. Come on, out in the yard."

"Now?" Bryan asked. He sounded surprised.

"Now," Dad said. "Get
your bat and come on."

Dad headed out for the yard. Bryan eased
Brewster's head off his lap and picked up his
big stick and headed after Dad.

Brewster got up and shook himself and
followed. I followed Brewster and Bryan.
The goslings followed me.

Of course.

We went out in the backyard and Bryan
and Dad started playing a game I have seen
before. It's called Hit-a-Ball-With-a-Stick-
So-Lily-Can-Chase-It.

Dad threw the ball and Bryan swung the

stick. But he missed the ball. It thudded into the grass.

I knew what to do! I ran after the ball. The goslings ran after me. Brewster sat and watched us all.

Bryan got to the ball before I did, so he won that time.

"Again," Dad said. Bryan threw the ball back to him. They tried this game a few more times. Each time Bryan swung his stick, he missed the ball. Each time he got to pick it up before I did, which wasn't as much fun as the other way around. Bryan seemed to feel the same way.

"See?" he said to Dad. His shoulders slumped. His voice was low.

"I do see," Dad replied. "You're looking at the wrong thing."

"Huh?" Bryan asked.

"You watch the ball when I throw it, but as

you swing, you change to looking at the bat. Keep your eye on the ball."

Bryan threw the ball to Dad. Dad threw it back. Bryan swung the stick again.

He hit the ball! Now we were really playing. The ball sailed toward the fence. I ran after it. The goslings ran after me. And then something amazing happened. Something I had never seen before.

Brewster ran. He heaved himself up and lumbered across the yard. He wanted the ball! It hit the fence and bounced off, right at him, and he scooped it up!

I stopped running. Gertrude thumped into my rump. The other goslings piled into her.

Brewster had gotten to the ball first!

But he didn't understand how to play this game at all. When you get the ball, you are supposed to run around the yard with it so that people chase you. Brewster just trotted back to Dad and put the ball down gently at his feet.

"Good dog," Dad said to Brewster.

What is good about forgetting to be chased?

Dad picked up the ball and threw it back to Bryan. Bryan hit it with the stick again.

"Hey!" Bryan exclaimed. "You were right!"

Each time Bryan hit the ball with the stick, we all chased after it, Brewster and the goslings and me. Casey flew over and sat on the fence to watch.

Sometimes I got to the ball first. Sometimes Brewster did.

The goslings never got there first, though. Geese are not as fast as dogs.

After a while, Dad and Bryan sat down in the grass with their backs against the fence. Brewster flopped down and put his head in Bryan's lap.

I sat down and panted. Gertrude came and settled down between my front legs.

"Bryan," said Dad. "We've got to talk about something. I'm not happy that you lied. You

said you were going to be playing with your friends."

"I *was* playing with my friends," Bryan said. "Brewster's my friend. And Lily. They were here, so . . ."

"Bryan," Dad said sternly. "That's not the point. You can't mislead us like that."

Bryan nodded. Dad nodded, too. "I'm afraid you're grounded this weekend. Plus, you have to clean the garage."

"Again?"

Dad frowned. "What do you mean, 'again'?"

"I just cleaned it. Mom paid me."

"Ah. All right. You've got me there. But you're still grounded."

"Okay. Sorry, Dad."

Bryan and Dad stood. "Let's head home," Dad said. "I'll lock up inside."

Home! This would be my chance! I raced

across the yard after Dad and dove through the dog door into Work ahead of him.

Dad went around doing things to doors and shutting off lights while first Gertrude and then the others squeezed through the dog door and ran to be with me.

"Good night, Lily," he said.

He left and shut the door to the yard behind him.

I jumped up on the couch and put my paws up on the back of it so that I could look out the window. Bryan and Dad were walking across the yard toward the gate.

The goslings followed me. They flapped and scrambled and peeped and got up onto the couch with me. They didn't look out the window, though. All they wanted was to look at me.

My plan was working!

I jumped off the couch. The goslings

peeped in a panic. I tore across the floor. The birds fell and flopped off the couch.

I leaped through the dog door. The goslings were stuck inside!

But they weren't stuck for long. Gertrude poked her head out through the dog door and peeped loudly at me. I thought she was telling me to wait, but I wasn't going to.

Gertrude shoved herself through the dog door. I raced across the yard. Other goslings pushed through the dog door in a jumble. Bryan had his hand on the gate that led out of the yard. It was open a little. Dad was standing next to him.

I ran as hard as I could for the gate. "Whoa, Lily, what're you doing?" Bryan asked. He started to swing the gate shut.

Too slow! I was through!

"Lily! Come!" Dad called.

"Lily!" Bryan shouted.

The geese peeped and peeped. But they were all too late. No one could stop me!

I ran right through the field. I ran straight for Home.

9

Home! I galloped across the field, down the sidewalk, up the steps. I shoved myself through the dog door. I tore down the hallway to Maggie Rose's room.

My girl was on her bed, reading a book. My girl!

I jumped on the bed. The quilt bounced under my paws and stuffed animals flew off the bed as I wagged and jumped and whined with pure happiness.

Maggie Rose laughed as I threw myself on her and licked her face and her neck and her hands. I'd been apart from my girl for way too long.

Maggie Rose was still laughing when Dad and Bryan walked in.

"Did you bring Lily home for me?" she asked.

"She brought herself," Dad said, grinning. "Boy, she's smart! She got through the dog door and out the gate before we could stop her and before the geese could follow her."

"She really loves you," Bryan observed.

"That's what happens when you have a dog," Maggie Rose replied. "You get all the love in the world."

"I think Lily needs a break from being a mother to orphaned geese," Dad said.

"Will they be okay without her, though?" Maggie Rose asked. I wiggled so she'd scratch my belly.

"They should be," Dad said. "They'll be upset, but it won't do them any harm. They have to learn to live without her someday. In fact, that's what I'm worried about."

"Mom says that because the geese are imprinted on a dog, they might not learn to fly," my girl observed.

"She's exactly right," Dad agreed. "Not sure what we're going to do about it, either."

When Dad left the room, Bryan came over to the bed. He sat down and reached out a hand to pet me.

I gave him a few licks to share my happiness with him.

80

"What's wrong?" Maggie Rose asked him.

"I got in trouble for not telling Dad the other kids won't let me play with them. I'm grounded for the weekend."

"Good thing it wasn't Mom who found out; you'd be grounded for a *month,*" Maggie Rose replied.

He shrugged. "Yeah, doesn't matter. Brewster's like . . . my only friend," he said. "Ever since we moved, I can't make any new friends."

"Oh," Maggie Rose said.

Bryan sighed and left the room. My girl rubbed my belly quietly for a minute. She seemed to be thinking hard.

"Oh, Lily," she said to me. "What happens if we get the adoption fee and Mom still won't let Bryan adopt Brewster?"

That night I was so happy I almost couldn't sleep. At some point I awoke and for a moment wondered where the geese were. Then

I pictured Gertrude and Harold and all the birds wondering where *Lily* was. The thought made me sad.

I didn't think it was possible, but I missed my geese.

The next morning when I arrived at Work, the geese rushed at me and nearly knocked me over. Gertrude leaned into me and wouldn't stop, so that when I walked I was constantly bumping into her.

Of all the geese, Gertrude was my favorite. She really seemed to care about me—she would probe me with her beak and turn her head, looking at me with one eye and then the other.

The other geese all followed me everywhere and tried to climb on me when I stopped. The attention was actually nice.

For a while, anyway.

Mom, Maggie Rose, and I all took the geese into the backyard. They immediately charged into their pool. The only two things they cared about were swimming in the pool and being with me.

"I have an idea how Lily could help the geese learn to fly," Maggie Rose told her mother.

"Really? That would be great," Mom exclaimed. "The geese are old enough now that they should be able to fly. Their real mother would be able to show them how."

"You know how Casey the crow likes to stand on Lily's back? And then when Lily starts to run, Casey flies?" my girl asked. "I thought we could try the same thing with the geese!"

"Worth a shot," Mom agreed.

I was pretty surprised when my girl told me to do Stay and then put Gertrude on my back. The geese were much heavier now, no longer little balls of light fluff, and Gertrude's feet were much bigger than my friend Casey's, and felt flat, without Casey's claws.

The geese in the pool all stared in amazement. Because I was doing Stay, I held still as Maggie Rose crossed the yard. "Ready, Lily?" she called.

I tensed. We were about to do something fun!

"Lily, come!"

I ran straight toward my girl. Gertrude squawked and fell on the ground in a flutter of feathers.

"Oh boy," my girl said.

The geese all piled out of the pool and pursued me, of course. Even Gertrude, who honked in irritation. Mom followed them, shaking her head.

"Well, that didn't go so well," Mom observed.

Maggie Rose looked down at the geese. "Do they *have to* fly? I mean, what happens if they don't?"

"Then they can't migrate," Mom explained. "There are some geese these days who don't migrate anymore—they just hang around in parks or on golf courses all winter. I don't want that to happen to these guys. It's better for them to fly south."

"Why?"

"It's too cold here. If geese try to stay in Colorado all winter, they can't find enough food and they get thin and weak. Sick, too. Predators can take them very easily—coyotes, for example. They don't all die, but it is a real struggle. Much better for them to go to warmer places, where they can fatten up for the long flight back."

My girl seemed to be thinking hard. "What about if we just sort of throw them up into the air? Won't they flap their wings then?"

Mom nodded. "I'm ready to try anything."

"Lily, come!" Maggie Rose called, walking toward the far side of the yard.

I did Come. The geese all sputtered and honked, shocked that I was leaving. They made a lot of geese noises and then all ran to follow me. They didn't like Maggie Rose as much as they liked me, and they backed away a little when she came close to them. But they didn't run, and she was able to pick up Gertrude again.

Maggie Rose held Gertrude in two hands. Gertrude wiggled a little and fluttered her wings, probably thinking what I was thinking, which was that my girl was going to put the big bird on my back again.

"That's good," Mom said. "Just let her go, Maggie Rose. You don't want to throw her or anything. See if she'll flap her wings before she hits the ground."

Maggie Rose let go. Gertrude stretched out her wings and fell to the ground. She shook her head and sort of grumbled and waddled away from Maggie Rose. She didn't seem to think that Drop-the-Goose was a fun game.

I didn't think I'd like it, either. I hoped Maggie Rose would not get the idea of playing Drop-the-Dog.

Maggie Rose tried her new game with some

of the other goslings. They all stretched their wings wide and fell straight to the ground.

"They don't get the idea of flapping," Mom said. "They've never really seen a goose flap her wings."

"We could put a pair of wings on Lily," Maggie Rose suggested. "Like my fairy wings I wore for Halloween once."

Mom laughed. I wagged. I think that laughing is how people wag, since they don't have tails. "Well, maybe not that. But we'd better come up with something," she said.

"We'll figure it out," my girl promised. "Lily can do anything!"

10

That evening, Maggie Rose let me squeeze out the gate and blocked the geese, who honked in outrage. I went Home with my girl and sat under the table while the family ate dinner. This is one of my favorite things to do.

"I had to do a presentation in class," Maggie Rose told the family while she ate spaghetti.

"Oh? How did it go?" Mom asked.

"I got an 'A.' Want to see? I'll show you!"
Maggie Rose jumped out of her chair. She
hurried into the living room and came back
with a big piece of stiff white paper.

This was so interesting that I crawled out
from under the table. Maggie Rose did not sit
back down in her chair. Instead, she stood
by the end of the table, holding her piece of
paper.

Maybe this meant that Maggie Rose was all done with her spaghetti and would be giving it to me instead. That would be great!

"My presentation is called 'Why Bryan Should Be Allowed to Adopt Brewster,'" Maggie Rose announced.

Dad sat up a little straighter. Mom made a muffled noise through her mouthful of spaghetti.

"Point number one," Maggie Rose continued firmly. "Brewster is an old dog and nobody wants him. He's been living at the rescue for a long time, and it's sad. He needs a family."

Bryan was staring at Maggie Rose. He had stopped eating his spaghetti. Maybe I could lick his plate, too?

"Point number two. Brewster likes playing with Lily. And it's the only real exercise he gets. It would be good for him if he lived here and got to play with Lily more. Point number three. Bryan loves Brewster, and he would take really good care of him."

Mom put down her fork. "Thank you, Maggie Rose, but—"

Maggie Rose didn't let Mom finish. "Point number four. I got to adopt Lily, so it's only fair if Bryan gets to adopt Brewster. Thank you. That's the end of my presentation," Maggie Rose said, all in a rush. She sat down.

Everybody was quiet for a few seconds. Then Craig started to clap. Bryan quickly joined in.

Clapping is a funny noise that humans make with their hands. I don't know why.

"Well." Mom shook her head. "That was quite a presentation, Maggie Rose. But you know that the rescue has a rule. No one who works there can adopt a pet. Their families can't, either. People need to trust that we are finding the very best homes for the animals, and not just letting employees have them."

"Yeah, but you did let Maggie Rose adopt Lily," Craig pointed out. "And come on, you're a veterinarian and dad's a game warden—everyone knows this is the very best home."

"We made an exception in Lily's case, but . . ." Mom hesitated. "Bryan, I didn't even know you were interested in adopting Brewster."

Dad looked down at the meatballs on his plate. Maybe he was getting ready to give one to me.

"Yeah, I . . ." Bryan stopped to cough. "I didn't know Maggie Rose was going to do that. But she's right. I'd take good care of Brewster. And he's been at the rescue for forever."

Mom looked at Dad. "James, what do you think?"

Dad looked at Maggie Rose and then at Bryan.

"It was an excellent presentation," he said.

"I'm proud of you, Maggie Rose. Still, decisions about the animals at the rescue are up to your mom, guys. All I'll say is—Brewster's a great dog. I'd be glad to have him here. But it's Mom who gets to make the call."

"I have to set an example for the staff," Mom said. "I have to follow the rules. That's only fair."

Bryan slumped a little.

"Anyway Bryan, even if Mom said you could adopt Brewster because it's only fair since Maggie Rose adopted Lily, there's still the adoption fee," Craig pointed out.

Mom nodded. "That's true."

"That's the one rule Mom can't break. And there's no way you could raise that kind of money," Craig told his brother.

"But if he could get the money somehow . . ." Maggie Rose suggested.

"It's too much—he can't do it," Craig insisted.

Dad was watching this conversation very carefully, probably wondering when we were going to discuss giving a good dog a meatball or two.

"Bryan," Mom said. "Taking care of a dog is a lot of work. You'd have to feed Brewster, walk him, pick up his poop in the yard. Every day."

Bryan was sitting up straighter now. I could feel the excitement in him.

"Yes," Bryan said. "Yes, I know, I get it! I'll do everything."

Mom looked as if she were thinking hard. Her face was all frowny. You'd never catch a dog with an expression like that.

"I think it would be a good thing for Bryan, to save his money for something important instead of just spending it on nothing," Dad ventured carefully.

Mom nodded. "All right. Yes, Bryan. If you somehow manage to save the two hundred dollars, you may adopt Brewster."

Mom looked startled when my girl, Craig, and Bryan all burst into happy smiles.

"Yes!" Craig exclaimed.

After dinner, Maggie Rose and Craig and Bryan all went into Bryan's room. I went, too, of course. Bryan had thin pieces of paper and round bits of metal scattered all over his bed.

"I've got a hundred and thirty-five dollars," he said. "This is taking forever. I've been washing cars and raking leaves and stuff."

"You'll get there," Craig said. "I'm helping my friend Roy stack firewood tomorrow—you can have my money from that."

"And I get paid for cleaning out the cat cages at the rescue—you can have that," my girl volunteered.

Bryan looked hopeful. "Do you really think this is going to work?"

The days started to turn a little colder, especially in the evenings. In the mornings Maggie Rose would pet me and say, "School," and then go away, which was very sad.

Bryan said "school," too, and seemed even sadder than I was. "With school I can't do extra jobs during the day. I'm still fifty dollars short," he complained to my girl. "At this rate, I'm never going to get to adopt Brewster."

After Maggie Rose and her brothers left,

Mom and I always went to Work, where I had friends.

I was usually happy to see the geese at first, but after a while became a little weary of them constantly following me. The birds made noises all the time, like a dog with his head hanging out the window. Brewster always stirred at the honking and glared at me, as if expecting that I could figure out how to make them stop.

I was never tired of being with my girl, but a bird is not a Maggie Rose. Sometimes a dog wants to be able to lie down without geese on her face.

Maggie Rose usually came in through the door that led to the yard. She'd drop her backpack on the floor and kneel down so I could kiss her and let her know that it had been a long, long time since we'd been together.

Then we'd go out into the yard, me and my girl and the geese.

My friend Casey would come by every now and again. He'd land on the grass and take off and the geese would watch him very closely. They'd flap and flap, but they wouldn't fly.

One day Mom and Dad came out to watch the geese play Flap-Our-Wings.

"I don't think they're going to get it in time to migrate," Mom said with a sigh. "We'll have to find a wildlife park somewhere that can take them."

"Craig says they have to run when they flap," Maggie Rose said. "Otherwise they won't get off the ground."

"Probably true," Dad observed.

"Well . . . I have one last idea," Maggie Rose said. "Mom, when I call, open the gate, okay?"

I was distressed when, moments later, my girl slipped out the gate, shutting it behind her. Where was she going without her dog? I went to the gate and whined and Mom followed me but didn't let me out.

"Okay, Mom!" my girl yelled.

Finally, Mom opened the gate. Maggie Rose was across the field, running. "Come, Lily!" she called.

Chase-Me!

Behind me, the geese broke out into frantic honking. I could tell they were playing Chase-Me, too.

I ran as fast as I could out into the field. Someone had cut the grass, so it was nice and short for running. "Come on, Lily! Come on, Gertrude! Come on, Mr. Waddle-puss! Come on, Harold!" Maggie Rose yelled.

I loved yelling. I loved running. This was the best!

I looked behind me. The geese were running over the grass. They had their wings out and were flapping them, just like they did when they played with Casey.

Gertrude was in front with her neck stretched out and her feet moving as fast as she could make them. Then an amazing thing happened.

Gertrude rose up into the air!

The other geese were doing the same thing. They were flying!

Maggie Rose jumped up and down and shouted with excitement. I barked, too, just to join in.

The geese flew in a wobbly circle and then came lower and closer to the grass. They landed and waddled up to me, honking as if they couldn't wait to tell me what they'd done.

Mom and Dad had been watching. Dad was clapping. Mom was beaming.

"Great idea, Maggie Rose!" Mom called out.

"Do it again!" Dad shouted. "Let them get used to how it feels to fly!"

Maggie Rose and I ran. The geese ran after us. They shook out their wings and flapped and flew. We did it again and again. Every time the geese landed, they seemed astonished and rushed up to me to tell me all about it. Maggie Rose would gasp and I would pant and we would run some more.

It was wonderful!

I didn't see why we should ever stop,

but after a while Maggie Rose told me to do Come and we all went back into the yard. Mom shut the gate. Maggie Rose flopped down on the grass and breathed in great big breaths.

I licked her face and lay down next to her. The geese piled up around us. Gertrude didn't join in, though. She went to sit in a pile of straw in a corner of the yard.

"Oh, what a relief," Mom said.

The people all seemed happy. That's what Chase-Me does. It makes everybody happy.

Maggie Rose sat up.

"It's funny Gertrude is over there," she said. "She always wants to be right next to Lily."

"Are you sure that's Gertrude?" Dad asked. "They all look alike to me."

"Of course it is," Maggie Rose said. She got up and went over to the corner where Gertrude was sitting in her straw. She gasped.

"Mom! Dad! Come look!" she called out.

I jumped up, shoving a goose off one front paw, and hurried over to see if my girl needed me.

"Look what Gertrude's done!" Maggie Rose said. She was pointing into the straw.

I stuck my nose where she was pointing, right under Gertrude. Gertrude got up and shook herself and waddled away.

In the straw where she had been sitting was a small, smooth egg.

The next day, Maggie Rose and Bryan and I went to visit Mrs. Swanson. Maggie Rose carried a small sack.

We arrived at Mrs. Swanson's house and Maggie Rose rang the doorbell. Mrs. Swanson opened the door.

"Lily and I have something for you, Mrs. Swanson," Maggie Rose said.

She was grinning. Mrs. Swanson looked

puzzled. My girl handed her the bag and Mrs. Swanson opened it and looked inside.

"Oh my," she said. "Oh my! Oh my!"

"Gertrude just laid it. It's a fall egg for your collection!" Maggie Rose told her, beaming.

"Of course it is!" Mrs. Swanson said. "Come in, come in."

We went in the house and Mrs. Swanson took a small egg out of the paper bag. She put it on the shelf with the other eggs. She did not seem to think of giving a good dog anything to eat.

"How much should I pay you for the egg?" Mrs. Swanson asked.

My girl looked surprised. "Oh, nothing," she said. "It's a present!"

"Oh, no, I can't take it as a present," Mrs. Swanson said. "No, that wouldn't be right at all. I'll give you exactly what I paid for the last one I bought. A farmer found it, and he knew I liked geese, so he offered it to me.

That was ten years ago! That's how rare fall eggs are!"

"Oh," said Maggie Rose. "Well, I guess that sounds fair."

Mrs. Swanson went into another room and came back with a handful of the thin pieces of paper that Bryan seemed to like so much these days.

"Here you go!" she said.

Maggie Rose's mouth dropped open.

"But I can't . . . but that's . . ." she stammered.

"I won't have it any other way," said Mrs. Swanson firmly. She pushed the pieces of paper into Maggie Rose's hands.

Maggie Rose looked up at her with a big, wide grin.

"I have to find Bryan!" she said.

Maggie Rose ran all the way Home, and of course I ran with her. She burst into the house, shouting, "Bryan! Bryan!"

I barked, because obviously we were being loud and that was fun.

Bryan and Craig came down the stairs and into the living room.

"What's the big deal? Why are you yelling?" Bryan asked.

Maggie Rose shoved the pieces of paper into his hands. "Look what Mrs. Swanson paid for Gertrude's egg!"

"Is it enough?" Craig demanded.

Bryan ran upstairs. He ran down again with more of that paper in his hands, plus a jar full of clinking pieces of metal.

He dumped the metal out on the dining room table and spread the pieces of paper out, too. He mumbled. Maggie Rose wiggled and jumped from foot to foot. Bryan looked up.

"Well? Well?" Craig pressed. "Is it enough or not?"

"Tell us, Bryan!" Maggie Rose urged.

Whatever was going on had everyone

as anxious as I
always felt when my
girl was getting ready to put
food in my bowl.

"Two hundred and three dollars and eighty
eight cents," Bryan shouted.

"Let's go!" Craig said.

Craig and Bryan and Maggie Rose and I all
ran across the field to Work. Mom was sitting at a desk in the small room called Mom's
Office. We burst in.

"Here!" he said. "I have it all. Maggie Rose
and Craig helped."

"So did Lily and Gertrude!" my girl added, beaming.

Bryan put the paper and the metal bits on Mom's desk.

Mom sorted through them. Then she looked up. "I don't know how you did this in such a short period of time, Bryan. But it's all here. The adoption fee has been paid. Congratulations. Brewster is yours." Mom smiled.

Bryan ran out into the room with the kennels and opened Brewster's. Brewster got up and groaned and stretched and came over to Bryan. He wagged his tail slowly but steadily.

The geese, of course, came to huddle around me and honk at me as if they were dogs and I were their person. I shook them off.

Bryan knelt down and put his arms around Brewster.

"I kept my promise," he whispered. "You're

my dog now, Brewster. I'll love you for the rest of your life."

After that day, Brewster and I did Work and then he came to Home to be with us! It was very nice to have another dog around. Brewster and I could chase balls in the backyard together. When my girl was busy, I could find Brewster. He was usually napping, so I would curl up with him and nap, too, without geese.

Brewster really is good at naps.

A few weeks after Brewster came Home, Dad and Maggie Rose and the geese and I all climbed into the car to take a car ride together! We drove up into the mountains.

I rode in the back seat with my girl, of course. The geese went in a crate in the back.

"Are you sure the geese are ready to fly south already?" Maggie Rose asked. "They've just barely learned how to fly!"

From the front seat, Dad nodded. "I know," he said. "But it's the time when the geese leave, so we just have to hope Gertrude and the rest are ready."

We stopped in a place high in the mountains, near a big lake. There were geese out on that lake—big ones! Grown-up geese! They seemed restless and kept lifting up from the water for short flights and then splashing back down again.

"See? Getting ready

to migrate," Dad said, watching them. "We came at just the right time."

Dad lifted the crate down from the back of the truck and set it on the ground. He opened it. The geese streamed out, honking and flapping and looking around with interest.

One goose—she was female, I could smell—paddled close to where we stood. When she saw and heard our geese, her long neck stretched out and her head lifted.

"Could that be her? The geese's mother?" Maggie Rose asked Dad.

Dad shrugged. "No way to tell. She's certainly interested in the young ones, but we just can't know for sure."

"Come on, Lily, follow me!" Maggie Rose said.

13

Maggie Rose led me down a short path to the lake.

The geese followed me. Dad followed the geese. We all arrived at the lake, and the geese waded in. They shook out their feathers and flapped, but they didn't fly. They paddled, just as they did in the small pool back Home.

But this was not a small pool. This was a very large lake.

The geese headed out toward the middle of the lake. They seemed very excited, and looked back at me often to see if I would join them.

I don't know how to paddle. To me, paddling is not a dog thing.

I stood next to my girl on the shore. "They're doing it, Lily. They're doing it!" Maggie Rose whispered.

The grown-up bird who'd seemed so

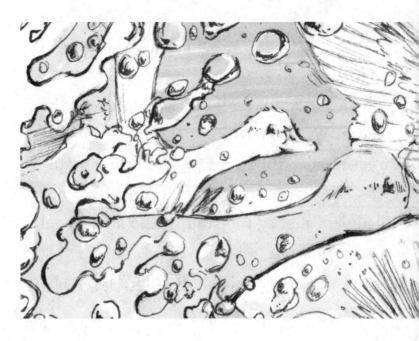

interested in my friends was still close by. She met the younger geese in the middle of the lake, and there was a lot of honking and splashing and flapping of wings.

"That's the mother. I'm sure it's their mother!" Maggie Rose said, clapping her hands.

"Might be," Dad said. "Come on, let's give them a little space."

We went back up the path toward the truck.

A very strange thing happened when we did that.

The geese did not follow me. They stayed out on the lake, swimming in small circles and honking and flapping.

Other geese were gathering around, too. Some were beginning to take off from the water in short flights. They'd wheel in tight circles and land again. Sometimes two or three would take off together.

At the truck we found a big bench to sit on, where we could see what was happening on the lake.

"I think we're about to witness something wonderful," Dad said. "It's the beginning of their migration."

Maggie Rose held me tight.

"These geese will probably go to California, or even Mexico," Dad said. "Some head for South Carolina. Hundreds of miles. It's amazing. And they'll come right back to this

lake in the
spring."

And then, with a
noise that sounded like a large wind in the
trees, the geese were suddenly all flying.

The shadows of the geese in the air fell
over us. They were honking and we could
hear the sound of their wings. It felt exciting.

It felt strange. It seemed as if the geese—*all the geese!*—were playing Chase-Me, and I should play with them. But I couldn't play Chase-Me up in the sky!

I jumped off the bench. I barked a little as the geese circled, the whispers of their wings joining into a steady *whoosh*. And then some geese headed away, the sun behind them, and then the others followed.

And then they were gone.

I sat and looked up at Maggie Rose. She seemed a little sad, and I nudged her hand. Then I looked out at the lake, which seemed oddly empty now, with no geese anywhere.

I thought I understood something then.

For so many days, I'd been surrounded by geese. Geese had been behind my rump and under my paws and cuddled up into my fur. Geese had been everywhere. They had bothered me like a bad itch. I longed to get away from them.

Then we came here, where there were many floating geese, and now they were all gone and my girl was sad, which meant that the geese were gone. Gertrude and Harold and the rest of them had left to be geese with all their bird friends, and would not be coming back to Work to be with me and Brewster anymore.

And I felt a little sad, too. Now that they were gone, I realized I actually had grown accustomed to having them around. What would it be like to go to Work and not have them come running up, frantically happy to see me? It was as if I were a mother dog and they were puppies. When I was a puppy, I had loved my mother dog more than anything else. And then I went to be with Maggie Rose, and I was even happier.

It never occurred to me that my mother dog might miss me. I wondered if she had been sad when we parted, just as I was sad now.

Then I heard it. A slight noise in the air, followed by a soft *honk*. Maggie Rose lifted her hand to shield it from the sun as she looked up into the sky.

"It's Gertrude!" she cried.

It was Gertrude, who loved me the most. She landed elegantly in the water, right near shore, and my girl and I ran down as she swam over to us. She came up on shore and straight to me. She leaned into me as she always did.

"Oh Gertrude, you came back to say good-bye," Maggie Rose breathed.

Gertrude and I looked at each other. I licked her on her strange lips and she wiggled her tail. She honked very quietly.

I knew then that even though geese are birds and not dogs, they can love in their own bird way.

I heard more honking and glanced up. A line of geese trailed across the sky, all honking, their necks outstretched. Gertrude saw them, too.

With one last look at me, Gertrude turned and plunged back onto the lake. Within moments, she had lifted herself with her wings and had joined all the others.

My girl and I returned to where Dad was waiting by the truck. "Oh, Lily," Maggie Rose said. "I know you miss the geese. But it's the best thing. They'll fly far away and have a good winter somewhere warm."

"And they'll come back," Dad promised.

"And they'll come back, Lily. They'll come right back to this lake. They might even come see us at the rescue."

"And they'll build their own nests," Dad added. "Let's hope they don't pick a planter in a parking lot."

We climbed in the car. There were no geese in the crate in back. But I did have my girl. I had Maggie Rose.

And I had Home.

Home was where all my family lived. I

loved my girl. I loved my Home. I loved my
family: Mom, Dad, Craig, Bryan, Maggie
Rose.

Brewster, too.

Gertrude and her nestmates are Canada geese. You can identify a Canada goose by its long black neck and the white patches on its cheeks. Male and female Canada geese look alike.

A Canada goose can weigh up to nineteen pounds. Their wings can stretch more than five feet across.

Canada geese eat grass, water plants, seeds, and berries. They will also gobble up crops like corn and wheat.

Most Canada geese live in Canada and the northern U.S. in summer. In winter, they migrate to the southern U.S. and Mexico.

Some geese who live near humans do not migrate. This can make the birds less healthy, and it can cause a nuisance for the people. A flock of fifty geese can leave two and a half tons of poop behind in one year.

It's best not to feed geese. Giving geese human food can make them sick. It can also encourage too many geese to stay in a too-small area and can discourage them from migrating.

Canada geese learn to migrate by following their parents. If a bird stops migrating, its goslings will never learn.

A mother goose usually lays four to seven eggs at a time. She keeps the eggs warm for twenty-four to twenty-eight days while her mate keeps watch nearby.

The goslings call or peep to get their parents' attention. They can even peep while still inside their eggs.

Goslings are ready for their first flight when they are between seven and nine weeks old.

LILY
TO THE rescue

LOST
LITTLE LEOPARD

Dedicated to the people saving animals at the
Humane Society of the United States.

 I was playing in the backyard with my girl, Maggie Rose, and my good friend Brewster.

Well, Maggie Rose and I were playing. Brewster was watching. Watching is something Brewster does a lot.

Napping is something he does even more.

Maggie Rose is my girl, and I am her dog. We were playing my favorite game in the entire world, which is Give-Lily-a-Treat. But Maggie Rose kept getting it wrong.

"Play dead, Lily," she told me. "Play dead!"

She had that treat clutched tight in her fist. I knew it was in there! Her whole hand smelled like chicken, and chicken is the best treat. No, maybe salmon. No, bacon . . . or peanut butter. . . . These are the sorts of things I think about a lot, but I never can make up my mind.

Probably the best treat of all is whichever one I'm about to eat, so I nibbled and licked at Maggie Rose's fingers, trying to get to that chicken-smelling thing she was clutching so tightly.

Brewster lay next to us in the grass. Brewster is a lot older than I am, and a lot lazier. He and I often go to a place called Work, where I visit animals and he sleeps. Then we go Home, where I play with Maggie Rose and he sleeps. He was interested in the treat, too, but not interested enough to get up and do anything about it.

That's how he is. I don't understand it, but there are lots of things I don't understand—like why Maggie Rose wasn't giving me the treat! I licked her hand even harder, trying to get my tongue between her fingers.

"No, Lily!" Maggie Rose told me.

Humans like that word: "No." I do not.

Maggie pushed me away a little. "Play dead, Lily!" she told me.

I stared at her. She had that tone in her voice that she uses when she wants me to do a trick, like Sit or Down or Shake. But she wasn't saying any of those words.

Still, when I do Sit or Down or Shake I get a treat sometimes. So I tried. I put my rump on the grass and looked eagerly at Maggie Rose.

She didn't give me the treat. So I flopped down to put my belly in the grass. Treat now, right?

Maggie Rose did not seem to notice how well I was doing Down. So I jumped up to give her my paw. Everybody likes it when I do Shake. Maggie Rose couldn't possibly resist and would give me chicken!

Except she didn't.

Brewster let out a long sigh and rolled over so that he could rub his back in the soft grass. He wiggled a little and groaned as the warm sun touched his belly. He closed his eyes.

"Good dog, Brewster!" Maggie Rose exclaimed. "Good job playing dead!"

Then she gave Brewster my treat.

I stared at her in dismay. Brewster got a treat for, what, taking a nap? Brewster takes naps all the time, whether anybody tells him to or not! It isn't a trick!

I don't think Brewster knew why he was getting chicken any more than I did, but he ate it. I jumped into Maggie Rose's lap and licked both her hands to get all the chicken taste I could. Since she was my girl, I accepted that she gave my treat to Brewster.

Good dogs have to put up with a lot of unfair things.

While I was working on Maggie Rose's hands, Mom came out into the backyard. I like Mom very much and normally I would run over to sniff at her shoes and see if she smelled like any new animals. Mom goes to Work every day and there are lots of animals at Work.

But I was too busy getting the last traces of chicken off Maggie Rose's thumb, so I only wagged my tail in Mom's direction.

"Maggie Rose," Mom said. "Your dad just called. He's working up in the mountains today, and he needs Lily."

"Why?"

"I don't know. He just said to bring you both, a bottle of kitten formula, and he'd explain when we got there."

Then Maggie Rose and Mom did the thing that people do sometimes, where they hurry around saying stuff like "Where's my phone?" and "Maggie Rose, tie your shoes, please!" I helped by following Maggie Rose closely so that she'd know I was always there if she needed anything. I am so good at this that she even tripped over me a few times.

When we got to the car, Casey fluttered down and landed on the ground. Casey is both my friend and a crow. He croaked up at me. "Ree-ree," he said. He says this a lot when I am around. It sounds a little like *Lily.*

"Can we bring Casey, Mom?" my girl asked.

"Better not. We don't know what your dad is doing, and I wouldn't want Casey to get in the way."

Sometimes Mom lifts the back of the car and Casey flies right in, into one of the cages back there. But not this time. Casey wasn't coming, and neither was Brewster, who was probably still lying down in the backyard, waiting for another treat to fall on him for doing nothing.

When I climbed into the back seat with Maggie Rose I sniffed to confirm she still had chicken. She did! I could tell she had treats making a delicious bulge in her pocket.

As we drove, I put my nose out of the window and sniffed as hard as I could. That's what I love best about car rides—all the smells that come gushing in the window, so many that they make me sneeze. Maggie Rose likes to wipe her face after I sneeze.

Soon the air coming at me was cleaner and colder.

I turned away from the window so I could sneeze on her cheek.

"Lily!" Maggie Rose sputtered.

I wagged.

The car stopped and Maggie Rose let me out. I squatted and made a puddle in the worn-out grass, then looked around, excited to be here even though I didn't know where I was or what we were doing.

I saw some big buildings, bigger than the house where I lived with Maggie Rose. Next to the buildings were big patches of lawn that had been fenced in. I hoped I'd get to go into one of those yards soon, and be off my leash and maybe find another dog to wrestle with.

"James!" Mom waved at Dad, who had just come out of a building. "We're here!"

He walked over to us, and I tugged on the leash to drag Maggie Rose closer so I could smell his shoes. He has the best shoes, even better than Mom's, with thick soles packed full of marvelous odors.

Dad gave Mom and my girl a hug and reached down to pet me. "You want to see something special?" he asked my girl.

Then I heard a scream.

W hat was that hor-
rible noise?" my
girl asked in alarm.

Dad grinned. "Come on, I'll show you." We
followed Dad around the side of a building.
Maggie Rose clapped her hands in excitement. "They're so pretty! So red!"

Birds! Big birds in cages, much bigger than
Casey. One of them let loose with a piercing
shriek and I blinked in surprise. Casey says
"Ree-ree" and makes other noises, but never

such a loud screech. "What are they?" my
girl asked.

"Scarlet macaws," Mom replied. "What

are they doing here, James?" She calls Dad "James" sometimes, which is odd because his name is Dad. Even a dog knows that.

Dad wore a disgusted expression. "The guy who lives here has been smuggling exotic animals. We came up with a warrant to arrest him. Those macaws must have been brought up from South America. They're wild, and they definitely don't belong in the Rocky Mountains. Macaws are jungle birds, accustomed to living in large rainforests. They wouldn't survive the winter—if we hadn't come along, they would have been sold illegally to collectors who would keep them in indoor cages for the rest of their lives."

I sensed that Maggie Rose was upset. I left Dad's shoes and went to sit close by her legs. I touched her knee with my nose so she'd remember she had a good dog with her. "Why would anyone do that, Dad?" she asked.

Dad sighed. "People will sometimes do bad things for money, Maggie Rose."

"It's why we need game wardens like your father, to protect the animals," Mom added.

One of the big birds let out another screech. I expected that someone would shout "No!" but nobody did.

"Wow," Maggie Rose exclaimed. She looked at Dad. "What's going to happen to the macaws now? Will they have to go to a zoo?"

Dad shook his head. "No, they're better off being released back into the wild, where they belong. We've been on the phone with the government in Veracruz, where there's a preserve, and we're going to take them there. But that's not why I asked your mom to bring you and Lily up here, Maggie Rose. The man we just arrested wasn't just smuggling birds."

"What else was he up to?" Mom asked.

"Jungle cats," Dad replied. "We got a tip

that he was trying to sell some tiger cubs, but that's not what we found. There's only one kitten here—a very scared little leopard who needs some help."

Dad led us to a tall fence with a gate in it. Dad opened the gate and we all entered a smaller yard. He shut the gate behind us.

The situation called for a ball or a squeaky toy, and I gazed expectantly at my girl.

"Where is it?" Maggie Rose asked Dad.

"See the pile of big boulders? She has a den up in there in one of the cracks."

"How big is it, James?" Mom wanted to know.

"She's just a baby, but I didn't really get a good look at her." Dad looked down at Maggie Rose. "Do you think Lily can get the leopard cub to come out? I really don't want to have to crawl in there after her. She's already scared."

"Lily can make friends with anybody," Maggie Rose proclaimed confidently. She bent down and snapped the leash off my collar. "Go get the leopard, Lily. Go on. Go!"

I was excited to be off leash and dashed around the yard. Whatever we were doing, it was fun!

"Lily, you silly," my girl called to me. I trotted up to her, thinking how much a chicken treat would improve things, but she made no move to dig into her pocket. She squatted down and pointed at some big rocks. "In there, Lily. Go see the baby leopard."

No toys, no treats. But my girl obviously wanted me to do something. When she gestured with her hand, as if throwing something at the rocks, I moved in that direction, puzzled but willing to play.

And that's when I smelled a familiar smell—the smell of a cat.

I know a lot about cats. When I go to Work

with Mom, there are usually cats there. They
live in crates, like all the animals at Work,
and people come to meet the cats and then, if
they're lucky, take the cats home. The *really*
lucky people get to go home with dogs.

That is what happened to me. I used to live
at Work, and now I live at Home with Maggie

Rose. It happened to Brewster too—he came home to be with my girl's brother Bryan.

But before the animals go Home with their new people, I play with them. I play with cats and puppies and grown-up dogs and sometimes with my friend Freddy the ferret.

Would I be able to play with this new cat? Sometimes cats are afraid of dogs, even a good dog like me or a napping dog like Brewster. This might be one of those scared cats, because it wasn't coming out. I could tell it was young, a girl kitten, and an unfamiliar smell clung to it—different than any animal I'd ever met.

"Go on, Lily," my girl urged. "Go find the leopard!"

Whatever my girl wanted from me would have to wait—I was too interested in the smell of the hidden cat!

I bounded forward and stuck my nose into the crack between two round boulders. Yes, she was hiding in there, and I could tell she was frightened and alone.

I have met lots of animals who are afraid of me at first. I know what to do about that, and how to help them calm down so they can play.

I thought about squirming into the space between the rocks, but I knew that would really scare her. Instead, I made myself smaller by lying down on my belly.

"Good dog, Lily," Maggie Rose praised.

There was a slight movement way back in the darkness. I saw the kitten hiding in the shadows. She was a pretty large kitten! She was staring at me. I wagged, still lying down. Doing Down was how I usually helped the cats at Work see I was not a threat.

Brewster had gotten a treat for lying down in the dirt. Now here I was doing the very same thing, but nobody was handing me a treat.

But wait . . . Brewster had *already* been lying down. He didn't get a treat until he rolled on his back.

Was that the secret?

I decided to try it.

I sprawled out with my feet pointing up in the air, wiggling and wagging in a perfect imitation of Brewster. Maybe now my girl would give me some chicken!

Mom, Dad, and my girl didn't move. No treats dropped from the sky. But I noticed something—in the shadows, the large, scared kitten stirred.

I watched her tentatively come forward. Seeing an upside-down cat walk toward me made me a little dizzy, but I remained on my back.

As she approached, the sunlight fell across her face. Her fur was spotted and her chin was a light color, lighter than the rest of her. She thrust that nose out of the rocks in order to be able to smell the good dog who was doing Brewster's trick with no treats.

I sniffed back. I smelled catness, but that other, unknown smell was something more wild. She did not smell like a kitten who curls up in laps. She did not smell like a kitten who gets treats from her humans for doing no tricks at all, like most cats.

The kitten sniffed my face all over. She moved on to my head and neck, coming even farther out into the sun.

I held still, because I could tell that the
kitten was still scared. I could see it in the
stiff way she moved, in her wide eyes and
her alert ears. She was ready to run away at
any moment.

The kitten squeezed completely out of the crack so that she could sniff at my rump and tail. She glanced up at Mom and Dad and Maggie Rose, but didn't seem to care that they were there—they weren't moving, which might have been why the kitten wasn't reacting to them. I've often seen that cats only get worked up about things that are moving. They'll ignore a ball that isn't rolling but they'll jump on one that is.

I could not imagine being the sort of animal who would ever ignore a ball under any circumstances.

I carefully flopped over so I was lying on my side. The kitten stared at me with wide, strange-colored eyes. I was pretty sure she would pounce on me—that's what always happened with new cats at Work. So I was surprised when she lowered her head, rubbing her round ears along my ribs, and then cuddled up against me as if I were a mother cat.

"Look at that," I heard Dad say.

"Poor thing has been all alone and is starving for love," Mom said.

"Lily is such a good dog," my girl said. I wagged at the sound of her voice saying my name.

"Do you have the bottle?" Dad asked.

"Right here in my pack," Mom replied. "Come with me, Maggie Rose."

Having the large kitten pressed up against my side was making me drowsy, but I noticed when Mom and my girl walked a short distance from Dad to a different part of the yard. The kitten picked her head up, but didn't do anything else as they both sat down in the grass.

"Maggie Rose, call Lily, but very softly," Mom said.

"Lily? Come here, now," my girl said quietly. I moved my head to see her more clearly. What did she want?

"Come here now, Lily," she repeated. Oh, she was saying *Come.* I knew how to do Come. I climbed to my feet, mindful to do it gently so I wouldn't disturb the kitten, who watched me alertly.

When I trotted over to my girl, the kitten didn't move. The humans went very still.

"If she goes back to her den, I'll have to try to catch her with a net," Dad murmured. "Hate to scare her so badly, but we won't have a choice."

Mom had something in her hand. I pointed my nose in that direction. It was a bottle! I knew about bottles. I once had some young pig friends who liked to suck on bottles very much. I could smell that this bottle had milk inside it, and my mouth started to water. I did Sit.

"This isn't working," Mom said worriedly.

"Lily, can you play dead again? Play dead!" Maggie Rose urged. "Play dead!"

I held out my paw for a perfect Shake. My

girl didn't grab it. "Play dead!" she repeated. I put my stomach in the grass—a really great Down! Still no treat.

Then my girl reached out and rolled me gently onto my back. "Play dead!" she repeated.

Oh, the Brewster trick! I pointed my feet at the sky and Maggie Rose slipped me a chicken treat. I loved Maggie Rose!

Upside down, I could see the kitten was cautiously making her way toward us.

"Oh, little one, it's all right," Mom said very softly. "Here, look. I bet you want this. Don't you?" Still sitting on the lawn, she reached out both her hands, the one holding the bottle and the one that wasn't. There was a tiny drop of milk clinging to the tip of the bottle.

I started to wag, thinking that bottle would make a perfect reward for a dog doing Brewster's trick.

Mom and my girl weren't moving at all. The kitten sniffed the air, approaching slowly. Soon she was there, pressing her face against my side. Mom lowered the bottle, and the kitten touched it with her nose.

I didn't want this kitten getting any ideas about my bottle. I stretched my neck out to sniff it too. I was getting my tongue ready to lick off that little droplet of milk when Mom pushed my face away.

"No, Lily," she said.

I really wished humans would just forget the word "no." It never makes anyone feel good.

The kitten was still pressing against my side when she put out her scratchy tongue and closed her mouth around the tip of the bottle. I watched, utterly dismayed, as the kitten made small sucking noises. "That's right, baby," Mom whispered. "You're hungry, huh? I know you're hungry."

Mom gently pulled the bottle back toward
her body. The kitten allowed herself to be
led, leaving my side. The next thing I knew,
the kitten was being cuddled on Mom's lap
and sucking eagerly out of the bottle, while

I lay there in the dirt with no milk and no treat at all!

Apparently I was the only one upset about this unfortunate turn of events, because Mom and Maggie Rose were both smiling.

"Great job, you two," Dad said from the other side of the yard.

"And Lily," my girl reminded him.

"And Lily," he agreed.

Since they were all saying my name, I decided to get back on my feet. I shook myself off, casting an unhappy glance at the kitten, who was still sucking away on my bottle.

Dad was making his way very slowly and carefully toward us. Suddenly he jerked in alarm. "Oh no," he gasped.

hat's wrong, Dad?" Maggie Rose asked.

"This is the first I've gotten a good look at her," Dad said. "That's not just a baby leopard. That's an *Amur* leopard."

Mom's mouth dropped open. "Are you sure?"

Dad nodded.

"What's Amur mean?" my girl asked.

"It's the rarest of the big cats. There are

fewer than a hundred left in the wild. That makes this little kitten very, very important," Dad replied. He turned and went out the gate and was back a moment later with a big plastic crate. He set it on the ground and opened the door, backing away.

"I know!" Maggie Rose said brightly. "Let's put Lily in there first. That way the leopard won't be as afraid."

"Excellent idea," Mom said.

Dad grinned. "That's my game warden girl."

"Lily, come!" My girl put me in the crate, handing me a chicken treat as a reward. *Yes!*

"Stay!" Maggie Rose commanded.

I've never been very fond of Stay, but I sat in the crate.

"Down!"

It seemed to me I was being asked to do a lot of things for a single chicken treat, but

I went ahead and dropped to my stomach.
Mom put the kitten in the crate. I sniffed
her milk breath. She immediately curled up
next to me, just like before.

Mom shut the gate. "All babies need to cuddle," she observed. "It's an instinct as strong as the need to eat."

I was not bothered when Dad picked up the crate, but the large kitten clearly didn't like it. She stared at me with wide eyes as if expecting me to do something about it. Dogs know people are completely in charge of the world, but most cats don't believe this.

When the crate stopped moving it was in the back of Mom's car. The kitten cowered when Mom opened the crate door.

"Come, Lily!" Maggie Rose called.

I jumped out but the kitten remained behind.

"Where are you taking the leopard?" Maggie Rose asked as Mom climbed into the front seat.

"To the zoo. There's a special place set aside for animals that need to be kept by themselves for medical treatment." Mom waved and then the car drove away.

Dad turned to smile at my girl. "Good thing I thought to ask you to bring Lily." He came over and scratched my back. I wiggled happily and panted up at him. Then I licked something very tasty off his left shoe.

I noticed some people, who I had learned to think of as friends of Dad, loading the big birds, one cage at a time, into two large trucks. It was a day for taking all sorts of animals for car rides.

"Let's head back, Maggie Rose. I've got a lot to take care of if I'm going to get those macaws back where they belong."

We climbed into Dad's truck. I sat with my head in Maggie Rose's lap and we started to move.

"Dad, will you take the baby leopard back to the rainforest, too?"

Dad shook his head. "No. Amur leopards are from cold areas—Russia and China. They're almost extinct. We can't risk losing a single one. She'll live in a zoo somewhere."

"That's a little sad," Maggie Rose said. She stroked my back. "Poor lost little leopard, living in a cage."

Dad nodded. "But not really a cage—it will be a large enclosure. When she grows up, she'll be able to have cubs of her own. We're trying to build up their numbers to the point where we can save the species."

"What will happen to the man who took the baby away from her mother?"

"That man," Dad replied grimly, "is going to spend time in a much, much smaller cage."

"She was so cute," Maggie Rose said. "And Lily liked her."

Dad chuckled. "Lily likes everybody. Thank goodness."

The next day, Maggie Rose and I took another car ride with Mom. Brewster decided to stay at Home, and Casey must have been busy doing crow things, because he was not around.

"Can I name her, Mom?"

"Who? The Rottweiler puppy we're going to rescue, or the leopard from yesterday?"

"Both!"

"The puppy already has a name: Jax. He's fourteen weeks old. Thankfully, he's had his shots, so we won't have to keep him separated from Lily."

"Okay. But I think the leopard's name should be Nala."

I glanced at Maggie Rose. What was a Nala?

"Perfect," Mom agreed.

"What happened to Jax's person?"

Mom sighed. "It's a sad story, actually. Jax was being fostered by a man named Owen, who is an army soldier. Owen fell in love with the puppy and asked if he could keep Jax forever."

"Foster failure," my girl noted.

"Exactly. But then Owen received orders to go to Korea for at least a year. He decided it made no sense to take a Rottweiler puppy, and he couldn't ask Jax to wait for him that long, so he dropped Jax off at his sister's house."

"That's horrible! Why would he go and leave his dog?" Maggie Rose demanded.

"Well, Owen has a duty to serve his country. Sometimes, that means sacrifice. But we all do things for the common good that aren't easy. Take your dad—he's going to Veracruz for almost two weeks. I'm sure he would rather stay home with us, but he needs to return those macaws to their natural environment."

"I'll miss Dad, but saving animals is the most important thing," my girl agreed.

"And sometimes saving animals is fun. Owen's sister is your friend Charlotte's mom. You can play a little when we get there."

We soon stopped at a house I had never smelled before. Maggie Rose and I jumped out of the car together. In the front of the house there was a tire hanging from a tree, and a girl hanging from the tire. She was leaning back so far that her dark hair brushed the grass. Then she sat up and waved.

"Hi, Charlotte!" Maggie Rose greeted her.

"Hi!" the girl answered. "My mom said you'd bring your dog. What's her name?"

"Lily," said Maggie Rose.

I wagged to hear my name, and the girl with the long dark hair flopped out of the tire and onto the grass. "Lily! You're so cute!" she said, and I ran over to lick at her face and sniff her hair.

Then I saw something over the girl's shoulder.

A cat! The cat was crouched under a bush near the house. She was staring at me with very wide eyes.

I hadn't really gotten to play with the large kitten the day before, so I was tremendously excited to meet this cat! I wiggled out of

New Girl's lap and bounded toward my new friend.

"Oh, Mia!" New Girl said. She sounded worried.

"Lily just wants to play," Maggie Rose told her.

"Mia doesn't really play. She's pretty mean. Like, *really* mean."

When I reached my new playmate, her ears went back on her head, her eyes squeezed into slits, and she hissed, her mouth opening on wicked fangs. I halted in shock. She lunged forward with one paw up over her head, and I scrambled back from her razor-sharp claws as they raked the air, and nearly my face.

What sort of game was *this*?

This was not a nice cat. This was a bad cat!

I backpedaled as Bad Cat came at me, slashing the air, hissing and spitting.

"Lily!" my girl called.

Bad Cat licked her paw and stared at me. I went to Maggie Rose, who had to be as outraged as I was at such behavior.

"Sorry," New Girl said. "Mia doesn't like dogs very much."

I followed my girl and New Girl into the house. Mom sat at a table and talked with another grown-up lady whose name also seemed to be Mom—at least that's what New Girl called her.

"We're going to go play with Jax!" New Girl announced.

"Okay, just don't let Jax inside the house," Other Mom Woman agreed. She looked at Mom. "Jax is a bit wild."

We crossed to a big sliding window. I wagged because I could see a young dog sniffing along a fence in the backyard.

"Ready? One, two, three. . . . Go!" New Girl said.

The door slid open, we all jumped out, and the door thumped shut. The puppy raised its black face and stared at me.

"Jax! You have a new friend!" New Girl called.

This dog was named Jax, and I could smell he was a young male—much younger than I had thought, because he was so big. He came running across the yard in the half-tripping way puppies have, and I wagged, ready for him to stop so we could sniff each other's butts.

Jax did not stop.

He crashed into me, almost knocking me over. He was heavy. As he jumped up on me, his legs pressed down and I squirmed away. I tried to push him over and he pushed back.

"That's a big puppy!" my girl exclaimed.

I tried to run away and Jax was right there, bumping into me, nearly plowing me over. He was clearly too young to know I should be in charge—I should be the one crashing into *him,* if I chose.

I finally managed to wrestle Jax onto his

back, but he was hard to pin down. He was very strong.

After a time, Mom slid the door open and came out with a leash for the puppy. I was relieved—playing with Jax had left me exhausted.

"Bye, Charlotte!" Maggie Rose called.

We left the yard through a gate. As we approached the car, I saw Bad Cat glaring at me from the base of a tree. Jax saw him too and lunged to the end of his leash, yanking on Mom's arm. "Whoa! Jax, calm down."

Bad Cat acted as if the sight of two dogs didn't scare her.

We went to Work. Along the way, Mom said, "I'm going to need to spend a little time training Jax before we find a home for him. Usually Rottweilers are very even-tempered—they were originally used to herd animals and pull carts like horses. That's why they are so strong. But Jax doesn't seem to have gotten the message that Rotties are supposed to be calm and obedient."

"Lily's obedient," Maggie Rose observed.

"Yes, she is."

My girl slipped me a chicken treat and I crunched it gratefully.

At Work, Jax was led, twisting and pulling at the end of his leash, back into the area where the kennels were. My girl and I played Book, where she sits with a dry, tasteless thing in her lap and tickles it. I do not understand why anyone would want to play with such a boring object when there are squeaky toys in the world.

I was soon snoozing, but lifted my head when Mom walked up.

"Maggie Rose," she said. "There's a big problem with the leopard."

"With Nala?" My girl set her book toy aside.

My girl was worried. I got to my feet, ready to help.

Mom reached down and smoothed back the fur on my head. I licked her fingers. They smelled like Jax. "Nala isn't eating. She's been hiding behind some rocks since I dropped her off. What do you think, should we see if Lily can help?"

On the car ride I could sense that my girl was worried, so instead of sticking my nose out the window or watching for squirrels, I cuddled with her.

Maggie Rose asked, "Is Nala sick?"

Mom shrugged. "I examined her pretty carefully, but yes, she could be sick. Or maybe she's just upset at everything that's going on. We don't know where she came from, or how she got here."

"Or maybe she's lonely," Maggie Rose suggested. "She's all alone."

"Or she's lonely," Mom agreed.

When we stopped and my girl opened the door, I was astounded at the mix of odors that drifted across the parking lot toward me. The very strong smell of many animals was on the air—mostly animals I had never sniffed before.

Maggie Rose loves all animals. Surely if we met some new ones, she would no longer be so worried. I pulled Maggie Rose right across the parking lot, heading straight for these smells.

We passed through some gates and soon were in the most amazing place I had ever been. Wide cement paths wound through the grass and trees, and lining these paths were huge kennels, all of which were filled with the intense smell of different animals. I zigzagged back and forth on my leash, towing Maggie Rose behind me, sniffing madly.

Mom turned away from us. "Let me just take this call." She put her phone to her face.

Maggie Rose pulled me over near a fence. "Giraffes! See the giraffes, Lily?"

On the other side of the fence, very large non-dogs were eating leaves from tall trees. *Extremely* large non-dogs. They were so big I did not want to look at them. Dogs prefer small creatures to play Chase-Me and other games with, like cats and squirrels. These animals were too tall to be of use to any dog. I knew their feelings would be hurt if I ignored them but it was their fault for being so big.

"Maggie Rose!" Mom called, "We have to go!"

om came striding briskly up to us, shaking her head. "I'm sorry, honey, this is all my fault," she apologized. "The animals here shouldn't be exposed to dogs. Dogs are usually prohibited from even being here. Lily's allowed because she's got a job to do, but we can't let her approach anything but the leopard. Stay on the path. You could look at the fish ponds, I suppose—I doubt the fish would be upset to see a dog. But everything else is off-limits."

"Okay, Mom."

"Did you know the zoo already has Amur leopards?" Mom asked as we walked along.

"They do?"

"They are a mating pair: Dazma, the female, and Hari Kari. They're old for leopards, now—thirteen. They have the most amazing blue-green eyes."

"So Nala doesn't have to be lonely after all?"

Mom smiled. "Well, it's not so simple. Dazma and Hari Kari would not welcome a cub who was not theirs. And there are so few Amur leopards in the world that Nala, when she's old enough, will join a breeding program at some other sanctuary."

I found a patch of melted ice cream that I licked up off the ground. What a great place!

"This way," Mom said. We climbed some steps—I found a French fry!—and entered through some doors and into a building that smelled like people and unknown animals.

We stopped outside a gate that was made entirely of bars set close together. Through the bars, I could see a small sort of yard with a high fence all around it.

A man with dusty pants was waiting for us there. "Hello, Doctor Quinton," Mom said.

"So good of you to come on such short notice, Chelsea," the man with dusty pants replied. "And this must be Maggie Rose and Lily. Which is which?"

Mom laughed.

"My dog is Lily. I'm Maggie Rose," my girl said seriously.

"Well, I do appreciate you bringing your dog, Maggie Rose. I hope Lily can coax our new little leopard to come out."

"I named her Nala," Maggie Rose informed Dusty Pants.

"Nala! What a nice name. We'll call her that for now," he agreed.

Mom swung the pack from her back and dug inside it. A moment later she pulled out a bottle that smelled like milk. I stared at it. What a delightful idea!

"Come, Lily." Mom took my leash from Maggie Rose and led me through that door. My girl and Dusty Pants stayed on the other side, but I could see her through the bars.

There was sand under my feet, and a pile of boulders in a corner, and a small pool. I ignored the pool because I don't like to swim and I *especially* don't like baths. I glanced at the bottle of milk, wondering when we were going to put it to good use.

All the animal smells floating past my nose were so overpowering it was hard to sort out one from another. But I suddenly realized I had previously smelled one scent in particular.

It was a cat. It was young. It was frightened.

It was the large kitten I had met the day before. Instantly, I had a very bad feeling that I knew who the milk bottle was for.

"Nala!" Mom called softly. "Nala, baby, come and see who's here!"

Nothing happened.

"Nala!"

I scratched at my ear so that the tags on my collar jingled. Then I glanced back at Maggie Rose, who was standing with Dusty Pants at the gate, her hands clutching the bars. "Do you want to let Lily see if she can find Nala?"

"Let Nala come out on her own," Mom replied softly.

It occurred to me that they were saying "Nala" because that was the name of the large kitten. This might be where she lived now—her scent was certainly painted all over everything.

I yawned and then blinked in surprise. Nala the large kitten was suddenly standing on top of a big boulder, looking down at us with her light eyes and spotted face. I wondered who had helped her climb up there.

"It's okay, Nala. Remember Lily?"

Mom bent down and snapped the leash off my collar. I stretched, unsure what we were doing. Was I supposed to go play with the cat on the rock? Or stay with Mom and the bottle?

I picked Mom.

Then Nala dropped silently from her perch, landing lightly on all four feet. "Leopards are amazing jumpers," Mom said over her shoulder to my girl.

Nala sat at the base of the big rock and stared at me. I reminded myself that this wasn't like Bad Cat, this was a kitten who liked me. Wagging, I wandered up to sniff her face and was rewarded with a swipe on my snout.

I wish cats would learn that jabbing a dog in the nose is no way to play.

Nala lowered her front legs to the ground and left her rump up high in the air, wiggling. I have played with lots of cats, so I knew exactly what she was going to do next. She pounced at me, but I was ready! I dodged to one side and nudged her with my head.

She toppled over into the dirt, lying on her back and kicking with both legs. I jumped on her so that I could gently chew her face and her ears. She shoved me off with her strong back feet.

Nala knew Wrestling! I raced around the

yard to see if she knew Chase-Me, too, but she didn't seem to. She just waited for me to run back to her and jumped on my back, hugging me tight with her front legs.

I flopped down so we could roll in the dirt, and then I looked up to see that Mom was sitting down on the ground. "Lily? Bring your friend over here. Come, Lily."

I obediently made to go to Mom, but Nala was right at my side, leaping up onto me, so I was a bit distracted. Eventually, though, we both closed the distance between us and Mom, and then Nala stopped, looking at Mom with unblinking eyes.

For some reason, Nala did not understand that Mom loved all animals. I went to Mom and nosed her and she petted my head, and then I looked pointedly at the bottle in her hand.

"It's okay, baby," she said. "Remember me?"

Nala solemnly watched me rubbing my head on Mom. When I flopped down on my belly and put my head in Mom's lap, Nala took a small step forward. Then another, and then another.

Maggie Rose made an excited sound on the other side of the door.

Mom held out the bottle of milk toward

Nala. By now I'd figured out who the milk was for—not a deserving dog, that was for sure. Humans often make decisions that make no sense to dogs.

Nala stared at the bottle. Her nose wiggled. Her whiskers trembled. She came closer and closer, and Mom pulled the bottle back a little at a time until Nala had to climb right into her lap to get it. I moved my head so Nala wouldn't step on it.

Nala grabbed hold of the bottle with her two front paws. She sucked and sucked.

When there are no treats being offered, a dog can always find ways to be happy. I ran around the yard. There was a stick in the dirt, and I grabbed it and shook it so hard it cracked.

Then the door opened. I looked up to see if it was Maggie Rose, but it wasn't.

Dusty Pants stepped through the gate, shutting it behind him. "That's amazing!" he marveled softly. "She wouldn't touch the milk this morning. I tried everything I could think of. Why does having Lily here make all the difference?"

Nala didn't even look up at him. I wagged, though, touching his Dusty Pants hand with my nose.

Mom nodded at me. "For some reason, my

daughter's dog just has the knack for putting animals at ease."

"I don't need to tell you how great this is. We were discussing force-feeding the cub, but that would only be a last resort. We need to keep her healthy, though, and she just hasn't wanted to eat."

"Mom," my girl called. "Can I come in and see Nala?"

The man and Mom exchanged glances. "Honey," Mom said, "we need to limit the number of people the leopard is exposed to. I'm sorry."

I spent most of the day at that wonderful place, called "Zoo." Most of the time was spent wrestling with Nala. Some of the time was spent watching Mom give Nala bottles of milk, and some of the time I sat with Maggie Rose on the other side of the gate.

When we arrived back at Home, Brewster

was there but Dad was not. I sniffed curiously, wondering where he was.

"I miss Dad, too," Maggie Rose told me. "He's in Veracruz right now, Lily. He's staying in a hotel right near the jungle, and he says he can hear monkeys in the morning!"

The next morning I went to Work with Mom and Maggie Rose. My girl went to the cat area and began cleaning cages.

Jax was so excited to see me he was whining in his kennel. Mom put a leash on the puppy, who lunged and twisted, trying to get at me. Remembering the sensation of having his thick body crash into my ribs, I remained just out of reach.

In the yard, Mom reached into a pouch on her waist and pulled out some delicious treats. Jax, now off leash, tried to climb on my head.

"Jax, come," Mom said.

I went obediently to Mom and did Sit. Jax bit my face. "Jax," Mom urged gently. "Come. See how good Lily is?"

We spent a long time in the yard. I demonstrated over and over how to do Come. Jax demonstrated how to chew on my body, climb on Mom, roll on the ground, and run away when Mom tried to put him back on the leash.

Once inside Work, Jax saw Maggie Rose carrying a cat. He went crazy trying to get to it, leaping and pulling at the end of his leash. My girl twisted away and I put myself between her and Jax to protect her.

"No, Jax," my girl said.

"Jax doesn't seem to know about cats. I'm surprised—I would have thought Charlotte's cat Mia would have taught him a few lessons," Mom said as she struggled with the puppy.

"Charlotte said the cat lives in the house and front yard and Jax always stayed in the back," Maggie Rose replied.

Jax didn't earn himself a single treat that day. I received several, however, which almost made having Jax slam his body into me worth the whole ordeal.

After putting Jax in his kennel, we returned to Zoo. Wonderful smells! I gobbled up a piece of hot dog I found in the grass. And then Mom and I entered Nala's yard. Maggie Rose stayed behind the bars. The kitten was hiding again, but soon after I sniffed around the base of the big boulders, she emerged from behind the rocks.

"The same thing happened," Dusty Pants informed Mom. "Nala hasn't eaten since you left yesterday. She wouldn't even show herself. I'm very concerned."

"I'm hoping our little leopard will get used to her surroundings soon," Mom replied.

Nala liked to play all the usual cat games—Hide-and-Pounce, Wiggle-Your-Butt, and Roll-and-Wrestle. I'm very good at these games, because I play them with the not-so-large kittens at Work. Those kittens are fragile and I'm always careful with them, but when Nala and I did Wrestling, it was like playing with a dog.

When Mom produced a bottle, Nala followed me over to her lap, but I did not want to sit and watch the kitten have more milk, so I trotted over to Maggie Rose. Dusty Pants was talking to her, and he opened the barred gate to let me out to see my girl.

"I'm going to take Lily to the fish pond," Maggie Rose told the man.

"That's fine, but otherwise please don't go anywhere else without a staff member or your mother," Dusty Pants replied.

My girl took me to a big bathtub. We stood behind a fence. "See the fish, Lily?" I knew what *fish* was, but couldn't smell any. But yes, if she was asking if I'd like some, I would be more than happy with that, though I like chicken better.

When we returned to Nala's yard, my girl sat on the cement behind the bars, and I put my head in her lap and prepared for a little afternoon snooze. She was quiet, too—we hadn't even announced to Mom that we were back.

I heard Mom talking to Dusty Pants. The
man cleared his throat. "I wonder if you'd be
willing to donate Lily to us."

Maggie Rose sucked in a breath, and I
glanced up at her curiously.

"Give Lily to the zoo?" Mom looked surprised. "That's a big thing to ask, Doctor Quinton. My daughter loves Lily more than anything."

"Just hear me out. When your dog leaves, it's as if someone has thrown a switch. Nala hides and won't come out. We need to get Nala to accept feedings from other staff members, which isn't going to happen without Lily."

"How long would this last?"

The man sighed. "I have to be honest. Once the program determines where they want Nala to go, we're going to need to make the move as successful as possible. I can't see us accomplishing that without your dog."

My girl raised her hand to her mouth, but she was not eating.

"That could be more than a year, Doctor Quinton," Mom objected. "You're saying Lily would move with Nala to one of the sanctuaries?"

"I wouldn't ask if this weren't desperately important, Chelsea. We have to do whatever it takes to help this little Amur leopard survive. The world can't afford to lose even a single one."

There was a long silence. "I'll have to talk to Maggie Rose, you understand. I really care about what we're trying to achieve—but this would be very hard for my daughter."

Maggie Rose buried her face in my fur. I did not understand what was happening, but I knew she was sad, and a sad girl always needs her dog.

"Oh no, Lily," she murmured. "Oh no."

8

Dad was still not at Home when we returned. My girl's brothers Bryan and Craig were, though. Craig talked to his phone, calling it "Dad." Then Bryan did the same thing. So the phone was called Dad now? Much of what humans do makes no sense to a dog, but this one was particularly confusing. How could Dad be a phone? How was a phone going to wear his wonderful shoes?

The phone was passed to Maggie Rose.

"Hi, Dad," she said in a small voice.

"What's wrong, Sweetpea?" I heard Dad's voice say. I sniffed the air but he was nowhere nearby. My nose couldn't find him anywhere in the house.

"I just miss you. I really need to talk to you," my girl told the phone that was not Dad.

"Do you want to talk now? You can take it somewhere private, if something's bothering you."

Maggie Rose shook her head. "No, I want to talk in person."

The next morning, Mom talked to her phone. She did not call it "Dad." Maggie Rose glanced up at her when she said, "I was afraid of that."

When Mom put the phone in her pocket, my girl asked, "What's wrong, Mom?"

"Nala refused to come out of her hiding place all night, and she's still in there."

"She needs Lily," my girl said quietly. "Doesn't she?"

"Why the sad look, Maggie Rose?"

My girl shook her head. "I was just hoping Lily could go to the rescue with me and play with Jax."

Mom smiled. "Let's stop there on the way."

At Work I was let out into the yard and a few moments later Jax bounded out as Mom held the door open for him. I cringed as I watched him barrel across the yard, knowing he was planning to crash into me. At the last moment, I dodged out of the way and the puppy fell and rolled in the grass. I jumped on him to keep him pinned down, but he was so strong he was soon wriggling away from me. He leaped and twisted and jumped.

"Look at that energy!" Mom said.

I was becoming annoyed with his habit of running at me at full tilt and then running *into* me, showing no restraint at all. At one point I actually chopped at the air with my teeth, letting him know I needed him to back away so I could rest from his constant playing. He sat and gazed at me, puzzled—considering, for the first time it seemed,

that there was some other creature in the world except him.

That didn't last long.

When I wearily climbed into bed with Maggie Rose that night, I nearly groaned with relief to be lying on soft blankets. I opened my eyes, though, when she reached for me and pulled me to her, wrapping her arms around me in a sad hug.

How could a hug be sad?

"Oh, Lily, I am going to miss you so much," she murmured in my ear.

I spent the next several days playing gently with Nala at Zoo and being crashed into in the backyard by Jax. Maggie Rose was doing School—the word means she leaves early in the morning and comes back with books in the afternoon. Craig and Bryan were doing School as well. So I spent my time with Mom. Every day, we went to the zoo to see Nala and give her a bottle. At Work I tried to let her know I would rather nap with Brewster, but she said, "Come, Lily," and let me out in the yard for another wrestling match with Jax.

Mom was still trying to teach Jax tricks for treats, like "Sit" and "Come." Jax seemed to think Mom was saying, "Climb on Lily and bite her lips." Whenever we were in the building, he was on leash and I wasn't. He pulled and strained to get into the cat area as we passed it. "Jax, you're going to be a good dog someday. Just not today," Mom told him.

I hoped someone would soon arrive and take Jax away. That happens a lot at Work. Animals live there for a little while, and then they leave to go and live with happy people.

I wondered which people the big screech-ing birds had gone to live with, and if they slept in their person's bed like I slept in Maggie Rose's. I also wondered why any person would choose to have a big bird with a sharp beak instead of a dog.

After a few more days Dad finally came back, and his shoes smelled better than ever! Everyone hugged him and was very happy to see him. Maggie Rose whispered something in his ear, and he nodded.

"I think I'm going to take Maggie Rose and Lily for a walk," Dad announced.

Mom regarded him oddly. She looked between Dad and my girl. "Oh?"

"Sure. Just a father–daughter walk with my game warden girl."

I was very excited to feel my leash click into my collar, especially since Jax was nowhere to be found. "You come, too, Brewster," Dad said. "You need the exercise."

Brewster likes to stop at almost every tree and lift his leg, so we walked very slowly down the sidewalk, pausing often.

"What's on your mind, Maggie Rose?"

"I really missed you, Dad."

"I missed you, too, honey."

"Something happened while you were gone."

Dad looked down at her and lifted his eyebrows. "Oh?"

I politely sniffed where Brewster had just marked.

"Nala can't live without Lily. Everyone says so. She doesn't eat or even come out. And Doctor Quinton at the zoo says they need to adopt Lily and take her away to go live somewhere until Nala is grown up. Which could take a year!"

I sensed the distress coming off my girl, and gazed up at her in concern.

"Oh, Maggie Rose, I'm so sorry that you've been carrying this all by yourself. Why didn't you talk to Mom?"

"Because . . . because you're the game warden. This should be your decision."

"Oh." Dad stopped and bent over so he could look at my girl with serious eyes. "Maggie Rose, Lily is your dog. This isn't a decision for me to make."

My girl's hand came down to touch me. Even her fingers were sad. I licked them.

"Is Nala really that important, Dad?"

They resumed walking again. Brewster took this as a sign that he should lift his leg on a fence.

"Every Amur leopard is important, Maggie Rose, because there are so few left. We don't know where she was stolen from, and so far the man we have under arrest isn't talking. But if we don't build up their population, we're going to lose them, and that would be a loss for all the world."

Maggie Rose bit her lip. "Then I know what I have to do."

We walked in silence for a long time. Finally Dad said, "What do you mean by that, Maggie Rose?"

"You left us to go to the jungle to free the macaws, because that's your duty, even though it was a sacrifice to travel all that way and be away from your family. Like a soldier doing his duty and asking Mom to find a home for Jax. And this is the most important duty of all, because Nala won't survive without Lily. So even though she could be gone for more than a year, I have to let her go."

"That's my game warden girl," Dad replied softly. He put his arm around her, and she put her arm around me.

Maggie Rose was crying, though I had no idea why. I licked her face and she hugged me for a long time.

Later, the family all sat at the big table and ate, and I squeezed myself between Maggie Rose's legs and Bryan's, since they are the ones who drop bits of food most often.

"The macaws handled the travel very well," Dad said. "They're back in the rainforest and I think they'll be fine."

Bryan let a bit of bread fall to the floor, and I pounced on it.

"That's wonderful. And Bryan, stop feeding Lily at the table," Mom said.

I heard "Bryan" and "Lily" and wagged

happily. Yes, I loved Bryan at the dinner table very much.

"So," Mom said carefully, "how was your
walk?"

Nobody answered.

"Maggie Rose? Why are you so quiet this evening?" Mom wanted to know.

More silence. Dad cleared his throat. "I think Maggie Rose has something important she wants to tell us."

My girl was sad. I hurried to her legs and pressed against them, so she'd know her dog was near.

"I know what Doctor Quinton said," Maggie Rose finally replied.

"What do you mean?" Mom asked.

"He said that Nala can't live without Lily. That we need to give Lily to the zoo so Nala will eat, and that when Nala gets old enough to go be in the program, Lily needs to go with her for a while."

"I didn't realize you overheard us. Why didn't you say something, Maggie Rose?"

"I needed to talk to a game warden," Maggie Rose explained.

"I see," Mom said.

"So if it's Lily's duty to go live with Nala, she can go. But when Nala can live without my dog, Lily comes home," my girl declared. "Okay?"

There was a long silence. "Wow," Craig said.

I could feel everyone being worried and unhappy and I did not know what to do about it.

"Oh, Maggie Rose," Mom finally said with a sigh.

After the day that Dad and his shoes came back, I started spending a lot more time at Zoo with Nala.

Maggie Rose didn't always come—usually on days when everyone said "School." On those days I would only see Maggie Rose for a little while in the morning, and then a few hours before dinner and in the evenings. Both times she seemed sad. Even when I grabbed one of my favorite toys out from under her bed—an old pair of Craig's socks tied together—and shook it in her face, she didn't smile like she normally did.

Jax, on the other hand, was *full* of energy. Every day he seemed bigger than he was the day before. And he still crashed into me as if he couldn't figure out how to stop.

"Jax went after a cat in a crate yesterday," Mom told Dad after my girl and her brothers left to do School. "We were processing an adoption and the woman put the crate down just as I was bringing Jax in from the yard. He went completely wild on me, trying to get through the bars."

"Some dogs just don't understand that cats can defend themselves," Dad replied.

"Jax sort of doesn't understand *anything*. He loves Lily, though."

At Zoo Nala and I played all the usual cat games, and we almost always ended up doing Curl-Up-with-Lily. After that, Nala would drink her bottle of milk. I pretended I didn't care that there was none for me. But I did.

People decide where dogs go and what dogs do, and right now they had decided I needed to visit Nala and play cat games and visit Jax and play dog-crashing-into-dog games. That was all fine, but I wished I could make my girl happy again.

My girl was so sad all the time that I gave up my post underneath Bryan's legs at dinner and always stayed right next to her, leaning against her for comfort. One such evening the family was eating vegetables, which I don't like, and spicy meat, which I do.

"I have news. About the Amur leopard," Dad announced.

I felt my girl grow suddenly anxious and I nosed her hand.

"We've got a home for her at the Land of the

Leopard National Park. She'll be transferred as soon as she's a little bigger."

"Is that close?" my girl replied quietly.

"I'm afraid not, Maggie Rose. It's in Russia."

My girl got up from the table and ran into her bedroom. I went with her. I pressed up against her and tried to make her feel better, even though I had no idea what was wrong.

The next morning, after everyone said "School," Mom took Jax and me out into the yard at Work. This day, though, we were both on leashes. Jax chewed my ears and jumped over me and our leashes were all tangled before we even made it out the door.

Once outside I smelled cat. Jax didn't, because he was too busy gnawing on my face. I shook him off as Mom unclipped his leash. "Jax, I don't think you ever met Mia."

I froze when I saw who was coldly watching us from across the yard.

It was Bad Cat.

Off leash, Jax scampered in circles, trying to entice me to play Chase-Me. Then he spotted the cat. Instantly he was charging joyously across the grass—planning, I supposed, to body-slam Bad Cat.

But Bad Cat had other ideas.

10

Bad Cat's eyes were slits and her mouth was open, her sharp teeth on clear display. Jax slowed because this was not the reaction he had been expecting. Suddenly, spitting and hissing, Bad Cat went after Jax, slashing at the air. Jax tumbled backward, fleeing, pure panic on his face. He was playing Chase-Me now, all right, but for Bad Cat it wasn't a game. Yelping, Jax tried to get away, but Bad Cat wouldn't let him. Finally the puppy ran and hid behind me, his tail down.

Bad Cat sat in the middle of the yard and smirked. She knew she wouldn't get any trouble from me, and Jax was trembling, peering around me at the threat.

"Now you understand about cats, don't you, Jax?" Mom said softly.

The next day Maggie Rose did School while I went to Zoo to play with Nala. Mom gave Nala a bottle, of course. "We're going to start you on solid food soon, little one," she told Nala. I hoped she was saying that the next bottle would go to a good dog.

After feeding the kitten, Mom went away and was gone for a while.

I was sitting on top of Nala and gently tugging at one of her ears with my teeth when I smelled Mom returning. With her was another smell, one that I instantly recognized. Nala pushed me off with her powerful rear legs, but I didn't want to do Wrestle more. I stared in disbelief at the gate to Nala's yard.

Oh *no.*

Mom opened the cage. She had Jax in her arms. He was wiggling with excitement and licking Mom's face and trying to tell her as plainly as he could that he wanted to get down and play.

Now, in all my time at Zoo, I'd never seen

or smelled another dog there. There were so many animals I couldn't even count all the smells that came to my nose, but I was the only dog, always.

Now there were two dogs here! What was going on?

Mom put Jax on the ground and he came bounding over for a game of Crash-into-Lily. Then he pulled up short.

He'd just seen Nala.

Nala, larger than Bad Cat, stared at Jax. Jax lowered his head and padded up to me, taking a long route that kept him far away from Nala. He nosed me, worried.

When Nala decided to investigate, Jax backpedaled away from her.

I decided to demonstrate to Jax that Nala was not like Bad Cat. I climbed up on her and instantly we were playing, Jax completely forgotten. I put Nala on her back and she wrapped her legs around me and twisted away. She jumped on me and I flopped over on the ground, doing Brewster's trick of pointing my feet into the air. Nala pounced on me.

Movement caught my eye. It was Jax. He was crawling forward on his belly, unable to resist playing, even if he was still worried Nala might be mean.

Nala and I both paused our wrestling and watched Jax. When he was close, I saw Nala's rump go into the air, and I knew what was going to happen next.

Pounce! It was a cat's favorite game. Jax backed away in alarm, but then seemed to understand. Nala just wanted to play. He carefully lifted a paw and that's all it took—now they were wrestling.

"Come here, Lily," Mom called gently.

I happily trotted over to the gate and Mom opened it. Then I sat and watched Nala and Jax tumble. Nala was underneath, but she

squirmed out and ran to her pile of boulders
and in a single bound leaped to the top. Jax
looked up at her in astonishment. Wagging,
he yipped, and then Nala pounced on Jax and
they were back to doing Wrestling.

I knew Nala well enough to be able to tell
when she was getting tired. As far as I knew,
Jax never got tired, but when he went to the

pool for a drink of water, Mom said, "Okay, Lily, let's see if this worked."

Mom went into the cage and sat down, a familiar-smelling bottle in her hand. Jax joyously dashed over to see her, and Nala, unable to resist an animal running, pounced on him. Together they landed in Mom's lap,

and then Nala caught sight of the bottle and went limp.

Mom had to keep shoving Jax's face out of the way, but she was able to give Nala the whole bottle. While she was doing so, a man came up to stand next to me to watch. It was Dusty Pants. He had on different pants, but they were still dusty. Mom stood up and came over to us while Jax and Nala resumed playing.

"Hello, Chelsea," Dusty Pants said.

Mom smiled through the bars. "I realized that we were all so happy with how Lily relates to other animals, we didn't even think about whether another dog would do. I decided that Nala would probably play with any puppy."

"That you were able to feed our leopard proves that you were right," Dusty Pants agreed.

Mom turned and watched the cat and dog

play. "Lily was the runt of the litter. I started thinking about what will happen when Nala grows up—she'll be huge compared to Lily. But Jax has thick legs and enormous feet— he's going to be big, big enough to wrestle with an adult leopard." Mom turned back to Dusty Pants. "And yes, the zoo may adopt Jax. I'll even come out and continue to train him. He needs it."

Mom opened the gate. She knelt and put a leash into my collar with a *snick*. She smiled at me. "I know someone who is going to be very happy about all this," she told me.

"Lily!"

It was my girl! I wagged and shook myself off and went to the end of my leash to greet her as she ran up the cement path to where I was waiting at the gate. Dad was coming up behind her, grinning. She dropped to her knees and wrapped me in her arms.

I sighed in contentment. I loved Maggie Rose.

"Dad picked me up from school and brought me straight here," Maggie Rose said. "He said you have a surprise?"

Maggie Rose stood up. I gazed up at her fondly. Dad reached out and grabbed the hand of Dusty Pants. "Hello, Doctor Quinton."

"Good to see you again, James," Dusty Pants said.

"What's the surprise?" Maggie Rose asked.

"Look who is in the enclosure with Nala," Mom replied.

11

Jax!" Maggie Rose gazed up at her mother in wonder. "You put Jax in the cage with Nala?"

Mom nodded. "They're going to be great friends."

"Look at the two of them," Dad said. "Finally Jax has met his match."

We all watched Jax and Nala play for a while. I wondered if I should get back in there and really entertain everyone, but no one opened the gate.

"All right, I've got to get back to work," Dad said.

"Me, too," Mom agreed. "Maggie Rose? Do you want to come help me? We just got in some guinea pig babies, and we have to figure out which are the boys and which are the girls so we can separate them—we don't want more guinea pig babies!"

"Can Lily come, too?"

"Of course! Lily's your dog."

Maggie Rose was not sad anymore! I'd done it! I'd finally made my girl happy!

"Let's let Lily in to go say goodbye to Nala and Jax," Mom suggested.

"Can't we bring Lily back for visits?"

Mom shook her head. "I don't want to confuse things. Jax is Nala's dog now—he's not going back to the rescue, or anywhere else.

Soon Nala will forget all about Lily, which is what we want. Jax will go to Russia with her when she's old enough, and he'll be her companion for life."

Mom opened the gate and I slipped inside. Nala and Jax had fallen into an exhausted heap and were cuddled up for a nice nap together. Nala picked up her head to watch me approach, but Jax didn't stir.

The way Maggie Rose was acting gave me the feeling that I would not get to see Nala again.

This happens to me sometimes. I will get to know another animal and even love that animal, but then my girl will be in a wistful mood and steer me to touch noses one last time, and then the animals have to leave for different places to live different lives.

It happened to me first with my mother and brothers and sisters. It happened to me with a squirrel that I knew named Sammy, and a skunk that Maggie Rose called Stinkerbelle, and a couple of piglets, and a lot of baby geese who thought I was their mother.

I don't really understand it. Sometimes I wish all my animal friends—Stinkerbelle and Casey and Nala and the piglets and all the baby geese (even though they were a little annoying at times) could just come Home and live there. We'd all have bowls in the kitchen for our own food and we'd all sleep in Maggie Rose's bed, cuddled up with her legs.

But that has only happened once. Only Brewster ever came Home and stayed. The other friends eventually all had to go away.

Probably that is because all dogs are more wonderful than all other animals.

Except maybe Jax.

When I bent my head down, Nala rubbed the top of her head against my cheek. Jax opened one sleepy eye and his tail twitched, but that was his only reaction.

I realized in that moment just how much I loved this large kitten. She had come into the world afraid, but she had trusted me enough to play and tumble with me like any other cat, and now she was no longer timid and scared. I felt a little like I was the mother that Nala never had.

And now we were leaving each other. Nala and I stared at each other for a long, long moment, and then I returned to my girl.

Maggie Rose and Mom and I left the building and walked on the winding paths. Usually I was on my leash for this part, but this time Maggie Rose carried me and kept holding and hugging me. I didn't mind too much, even when we walked past a bit of pizza on the ground under a bush and I didn't get to go and eat it. It was so nice to have my girl be happy.

"I didn't want to tell you until I had permission from the zoo to try it out," Mom explained. "I didn't want to get your hopes up, Maggie Rose, in case they didn't want to try another dog instead of Lily. And then there was the question of whether Nala would accept a Rottweiler puppy. But they act like they've been friends their whole lives. It went even better than I was hoping."

"So Lily can really stay at home with us?" Maggie Rose asked, squeezing me a little tighter.

Mom put her arm around Maggie Rose's shoulders so we were all in the hug together. "Oh, yes, of course. Lily can stay."

We slipped into the car, and I curled up on Maggie Rose's lap in the back seat. I was tired from all my playing and a little sad, too, even though I was with my girl. I felt that something had gone away.

But my girl had not gone away, and that was what was most important.

"I bet Lily will miss Nala, though," Maggie

Rose said, stroking my back. "It's like she's lost her baby, kind of."

"We will all miss Nala," Mom said from the front of the car, which began moving.

"Lily is my baby," my girl proclaimed. "Are you my baby, Lily?"

Maggie Rose reached into an open bag that lay beside her on the seat. She pulled something out. It was a bottle, and it was full of milk! Maggie Rose flipped me onto my back, Brewster-style, and pulled me into her lap. I went willingly, my nose twitching.

She put the bottle near my face and I grabbed hold of the tip with my teeth quickly, before she could change her mind.

The milk that squirted into my mouth was rich and delicious and marvelous, just as I had always known it would be.

Sometimes it takes people a while to figure out what to do, but they usually get there in the end. Finally, Maggie Rose understood that bottles were not just for large cats—they were for good dogs, too.

And I was a very, very good dog.

All leopards have spots. They are called rosettes.

Leopards look a lot like jaguars, but you can tell the difference by looking at their spots. Jaguars have a spot in the center of each rosette. Leopards do not.

Leopards are nocturnal. They hunt at night and sleep or rest during the day, often up in trees.

Leopards are the smallest of the big cats. (The other big cats are lions, tigers, and jaguars.)

A leopard mother usually has two to three cubs at a time. They weigh a little more than one pound when they are born. The cubs stay with the mother for about two years, until they are old enough to hunt for themselves.

Wild leopards are found in Africa and Eurasia. Amur leopards, like Nala, live in eastern Russia and northern China. They are named after the Amur River, which runs along the border between the two countries.

Amur leopards usually live between ten to fifteen years in the wild. In a zoo, like Nala, one might live to be twenty.

Leopards are amazing jumpers. Amur leopards have been known to leap up to nineteen feet in one bound—that's like jumping over three adults lying head-to-toe on the ground.

All leopards are carnivores and eat meat.

Amur leopards hunt deer, wild pigs, mice, and rabbits.

Amur leopards are very endangered. There are fewer than a hundred left in the wild.

LILY
TO THE rescue

THE
MISFIT DONKEY

For the wonderful volunteers and staff helping animals at PAWS Chicago

Maggie Rose is my girl. I am her dog. In my opinion, this means we should be together every moment. Being together with Maggie Rose means playing with balls in the yard. Or getting belly rubs. (I get the belly rubs, not her.) Or stopping in the kitchen for treats as often as possible.

The kitchen is the best room in the house. It smells amazing. Sometimes I just like to lie on the floor in there and let the smells fill up my nose and hope that soon food will fill up my mouth.

But I can't always be with Maggie Rose, because on some days she says "School" to me and then she goes away. That is very sad. I don't know why a girl would ever go away from her dog.

On those days of "School" I often go with Mom to Work, which is a building full of friends for me to visit. Brewster, one of my very best friends, is an old, tired dog who goes with me on those mornings. Brewster's person is Bryan, who is Maggie Rose's brother. Whatever "School" means, it seems to apply to Bryan as well, because whenever Maggie Rose says it, Bryan leaves, too.

But there are other days that Maggie Rose doesn't say "School," and those are the best days.

On those days, Maggie Rose lies in bed until I jump on her and paw at the blankets and stick my nose under the covers to find her face and lick her ears or her cheek or her chin.

"Lily!" she moans. That's what she did this morning. "Lily! It's Saturday! I wanted to sleep late!"

I understood exactly what she was saying: it was time to wrestle! I grabbed a hank of her hair in my mouth and backed up, shaking my jaws, while she shrieked and giggled. "You are such a crazy dog!"

On this not-School day, Maggie Rose ate toast and other things for breakfast while I sat by her feet and drooled. She saved a crust for me. She always does, and I'm grateful. Maybe someday she will save an entire slice for me. I would be fine with that, too.

Brewster followed me into the kitchen, because Bryan was not home. In fact, Bryan hadn't slept in his bed the night before. I could smell that just as easily as I could smell the fact that Brewster *had* slept in Bryan's bed. Brewster is very good at sleeping on soft things.

Once Maggie Rose and I were done with breakfast, we headed out into the yard. Maggie Rose found one of my toys, one that squeaks in a satisfying way when I bite down hard. She sat down next to me in the grass, holding the toy in one hand. With the other hand, she covered up my eyes.

"Okay, Lily. This is going to be really hard!" she said, and I could feel her move as if she had thrown something. "Find the toy!" she told me. She took her hand away from my face.

I could smell exactly where the toy had landed, so I trotted over to it and jumped on it and chewed it hard, so it squeaked and squeaked and squeaked. I brought it back to Maggie Rose, and she seemed very excited and pleased. Not pleased enough to give me a treat, but still happy.

Brewster was not impressed at all. He just lay in the shade by the fence. I know that he can be lured into playing with a squeaky toy if I jump up and down and shake it right in his face, but it takes a lot of effort.

When Bryan came into the yard, I thought maybe now we'd have a game of two chil-

dren and two dogs and one squeaky toy, but it didn't happen. Instead, Bryan scuffed his way across the grass to Brewster, who raised his head and wagged. You can tell that Bryan is Brewster's person, because Brewster doesn't raise his head for anyone else.

"Hi, Bryan!" Maggie Rose called out. "Did you have a good sleepover?"

Bryan flopped down on the grass and put his arms around Brewster. I can tell a sad boy when I see one, and so can Brewster, who immediately put his head against Bryan's side to give comfort.

Maggie Rose went over to Bryan, so I did, too. Bryan smelled like himself, and Brewster, and peanut butter.

"What's wrong, Bryan?" Maggie Rose asked softly. "Did you and Carter get into a fight?"

Bryan shook his head. Brewster and I looked at each other, wondering what was going on with our people.

"Then what happened?" Maggie Rose asked.

"Carter's moving. To *South Carolina.*"

"Oh," Maggie Rose replied.

"He's been my best friend since first grade," Bryan went on. "Then we moved here to this stupid new house, and I didn't get to go to school with him anymore. Mom and Dad said they'd drive me anytime I wanted to see him, but they're always too busy. And now he's the one who's moving, and I'm never going to see him again."

Maggie Rose sat cross-legged in the grass, so I plopped down next to her. Whatever was going on, it seemed like nobody needed a squeaky toy right now.

"I'm sorry, Bryan."

"Now my only friend in the whole world is Brewster."

Brewster perked up his ears. I was sure he could feel the waves of anger and sadness coming off Bryan.

"Well," Maggie Rose began, "you and Carter will still be able to write each other. And FaceTime and stuff. And maybe he could come visit in the summers! I read a book where friends stayed together until they were really, really old, like thirty."

Bryan looked away. "Not the same thing," he replied bitterly.

"So, what about new friends? You could make new friends," Maggie Rose suggested.

Bryan snorted. "Like that's easy. By the time you're in fifth grade, all the kids have best friends already. Nobody needs a new one." He got up. "Come on, Brewster."

I lay next to Maggie Rose as we watched Bryan walk toward the house. They went in the kitchen door. I was worried that he'd get some peanut butter in there and share it with Brewster but not with me. Maggie Rose was worried, too. I could tell.

"We have to come up with some way to help Bryan make friends, Lily," Maggie Rose whispered.

I didn't know what she was saying, so I wagged. Maybe there'd be peanut butter soon.

The next morning,
Maggie Rose and I
decided that the very first thing we wanted
to do when we woke up was to go visit with
Mom. Well, actually Maggie Rose decided
that, but I was happy to go along. Mom was
sitting at the kitchen table eating toast and
some other things, too.

I am always glad to eat a crust of toast, no
matter who gives it to me. So I sat hopefully
at Mom's feet.

"Good morning, Maggie Rose. Want some breakfast?" Mom asked.

"Yes, please, Mom."

Mom stood up and went to the counter and began clinking things together in a way that sounded very much like a good dog was about to get a treat.

"Mom?" Maggie Rose asked. "We're going on our trip today? Just us?"

"That's right!" Mom put bread in the toaster. I wagged at the smell. "Excited?"

"Yes." Maggie Rose nodded. "But . . ."

Mom stopped clinking things and turned. "But what, honey?"

"It's just . . ."

"Just what?"

"Just, whatever we're doing, can Bryan come, too?"

Mom straightened in surprise. "Bryan? I thought you wanted some mother-daughter time."

"It's just that Carter is moving away, and Bryan found out yesterday," Maggie Rose explained in a rush. "So I thought if we're going someplace fun, he'd like to go, and maybe he'd have fun, too."

Mom came back to the table carrying a plate of things that smelled delicious. She placed it in front of Maggie Rose, so I went and sat next to my girl. "Carter's moving away? I didn't know that. That's going to be so tough for Bryan." She sighed. "It's sweet of you to think of inviting him, hon. You've got such a good heart. Yes, I'll ask him. But I don't think we should bring Brewster along on this trip."

"What about Lily?" Maggie Rose asked.

Mom smiled a little. "Lily can come. In fact, it's a particularly good trip for Lily."

"How come?"

"You'll find out. It's a secret." Mom smiled more and took a bite of toast.

I was still sitting and being a good dog when Bryan came shuffling into the kitchen. Bryan always walks as if he's kicking dirt, even if there isn't any. "Where's Craig?" he asked as he sat next to my girl.

"Your brother's already helping your father with chores," Mom replied.

Bryan groaned. "Just great."

I watched them all eat and I noticed that Bryan put peanut butter on his toast. What a wonderful idea! Now we had two kinds of toast right up there on the table. I would love to spend the whole morning tasting first one kind of toast, then the other. We could all do it, and then we'd each decide which was our favorite. My favorite would either be the toast with peanut butter or the toast without.

"Don't you want to do chores today?" Maggie Rose teased him.

"Dad always wants to do chores," Bryan

replied. "If I do them too fast, he gives me more to do, and if I do them too slow, he gives me more to do."

"So . . ." Maggie Rose said slyly, "you want to do something that's not chores?"

"Yeah, of course." Bryan snorted. "Who wouldn't?"

"Like come with me and Mom?"

Bryan hesitated. "Where are you guys going?"

"It's a secret," Mom said, stirring the coffee in her cup.

Bryan frowned. "It's not going shopping for clothes, is it? Like new dresses or something?"

Mom and Maggie Rose both laughed. "No, not that," Mom told him.

"Then what?"

"Come along and find out," Mom told him.

All the people seemed to be having a good time talking. But none of them were saying my name, and none of them were giving me any toast. I flopped to the floor with a long, sad sigh, and just then Bryan flicked a bit of toast off the table. It was a crust with peanut butter on it and it bounced right off my nose! I crunched it right up. My *favorite*!

"Okay," Bryan agreed cautiously. "I'll go."

Then a piece of crust fell from my girl's fingers onto the floor, and I grabbed it just as quickly. It was plain, with no peanut butter. My *favorite*!

"All right, then. Put on some old sneakers, because they might get a little dirty," Mom advised. "Let's go!"

Car ride!

I sat between Maggie Rose and Bryan in the back seat. I licked Maggie Rose and gazed out the window, watching for squirrels. I saw a dog and I barked.

"Lily! Don't bark!" Maggie Rose told me. I felt sure she was telling me I was doing a good job of spotting a dog and barking to let it know I had seen it. The other dog didn't look at me as we went by, probably embarrassed because he didn't have a car of his own. I went back to searching for squirrels.

"Are we going to the zoo?" my girl asked.

"No. Not the zoo," Mom replied. "But there are animals where we're going."

"The game preserve?" Bryan guessed.

"No, not to the game preserve."

"So it has animals, and Lily is allowed to go," Maggie Rose said thoughtfully.

"Oh, I know where we're going!" Bryan announced. "To a farm!"

"Exactly right, Bryan. To a farm where Lily knows two of the animals."

Bryan frowned at my girl. "Lily knows some farm animals, Maggie Rose?"

Maggie Rose shook her head. "I don't think so. Like cows?"

"No, no cows on this farm."

Bryan lifted a hand that smelled marvelously like peanut butter. He scratched his head. "Chickens?"

"No chickens."

"Zebras?" Maggie Rose asked.

Mom laughed.

"Crocodiles? Anteaters? Giraffes?" Bryan guessed. All the humans in the car were laughing, so I wagged. People don't have tails to let others know they're happy, but laughter is the next best thing.

"Oh, *wait!*" Maggie Rose exclaimed. "I know where we're going!"

3

Bryan was staring at Maggie Rose. "So? Where are we going?" he demanded.

"To visit the pigs!" Maggie Rose replied.

Bryan looked to Mom. "Really?"

Bryan was smiling. It was nice that he was no longer unhappy. I thought of Brewster, at Home, lying on Bryan's bed, believing his boy was still sad. Brewster would be so excited when we returned and his peanut-butter-scented person was cheerful again!

"It's been a little while since we dropped off the piglets at their farm, and I want to check up on them," Mom said. "I try to follow up with all the animals that the rescue places, as best I can. And we don't get too many baby pigs, so I really want to see how Scamper and Dash are doing."

"And that's why Lily gets to come! She's friends with the pigs!"

I knew the word "pig," but could not smell one or see one out the window. It wasn't until the car stopped and the doors opened and I was allowed to jump down that I knew why everyone was talking pigs all of a sudden.

Several smells came to me at once on the warm air. Grass and clover and hay and lots of different animals. I sniffed hard and started to wag, because now I could smell Scamper and Dash!

Scamper and Dash are two pigs who are my friends. A while ago, they came to Work

to drink milk out of bottles and run around like crazy animals. We played and played, and napped, and then Mom or Dad or even Maggie Rose would give them more milk in bottles. But I did not get any of that milk, not even a little bit.

This happens sometimes, but not because everyone loves pigs more than dogs. People just make bad decisions now and then. A good dog has to put up with it, because dogs are better for people than a couple of pigs, even pigs who can run really fast.

I'm sure most dogs would agree with me on this.

I had already forgiven Scamper and Dash for getting bottles of milk when I didn't, so now, I pulled hard against the leash my girl was holding, dragging her toward their smell. We came to a fence made of long wooden rails with spaces between them. Mom and Bryan followed more slowly.

"Okay, okay, Lily, I'm coming!" Maggie Rose said as I towed her. "Wait! Lily, wait!"

I knew she was telling me that she was as excited to see Scamper and Dash as I was.

On the other side of the wooden fence were three big pigs. One of them was very big, and I recognized her scent. She was the mother pig! Her name was Sadie. But where were my little friends Scamper and Dash?

The two pigs that were lying in the muck

with the mother jumped to their feet and ran over to see me at the fence, squealing and kicking up dirt. They shoved their snouts through the fence, and when we touched noses I was amazed.

These big pigs were Scamper and Dash! They used to be babies, and now they were bigger than I was! But they smelled the same, and they were still very friendly. I looked up at Maggie Rose and wiggled impatiently. My girl just *had* to take me off my leash. It was time to play!

She reached down and unclicked my leash. "Okay, Lily!" I dove under the bottom rail of the fence, and Scamper and Dash lunged to greet me. We sniffed each other all over.

Pig is a very interesting smell, not like anything else in the world. It's wonderfully powerful and musty. Once you've smelled pig, you'll never forget it.

So Scamper and Dash were now bigger and

heavier . . . but did they still like to run? I took off at a gallop, looking back in hopes that Scamper and Dash remembered the rules and would follow. They did! My feet splashed and slid in wonderful, slippery, squishy mud, and my two pig friends and I tore up and down their pen together.

The biggest pig lay comfortably in a hollow in the ground where some hay was scattered. Sadie was sort of like Brewster, more interested in lying down than in a wonderful game of Chase-Me. When I ran up to her with my tail wagging, she sniffed my nose gently, but she didn't get up. She was so huge I wasn't actually sure she *could* get up.

That was all right. Scamper and Dash and I were busy enough. I found a scrap of old rope in a corner of the pen and grabbed it with my teeth. I shook it hard and danced with it, teasing Scamper and Dash, but it seems that pigs don't understand how to play Tug-the-Rope. Neither of them tried to grab it.

They did understand Dig, though. When I dropped the rope because I smelled something interesting underneath the dirt, they came to help me claw at the ground. With my paws and their hooves, we sent the dirt flying!

"Lily, yuck!" I heard Maggie Rose call.

I found what I'd sniffed out—it was a big chunk of orange peel that had been squashed into the mud. Then I looked over to see what Maggie Rose wanted.

She was wiping mud off her face and the front of her sweatshirt and shaking her head at me. "You splattered mud all over me, Lily!"

Bryan was laughing at her. "That's what you get for standing too close to the pig pen."

I dashed over to wiggle under the bars of the pen and pant up at her, wagging hard. It was so much fun here! I was glad it was making Bryan and Maggie Rose happy. Then I turned right back to keep on playing with Scamper and Dash.

Out of the corner of my eye I saw my girl stop wiping her face and straighten up. She turned and pointed. "Hey, look!" she exclaimed.

4

I was very busy with my pig friends. They smelled just like I remembered, and they liked to run just as much as I remembered, but not everything was the same. For one thing, they used to topple over whenever I jumped on them. But now they stayed on all four feet no matter what I did.

I was squirming under Dash's belly when an odd sound filled the air.

It was a low, rumbling noise, deep and loud,

ending in a squeal that reminded me a bit of the sounds Scamper and Dash made. I lifted my head and stared. Trotting up to the fence was what looked a little like a baby horse, but with shorter legs and a thicker body. He stopped and lowered his head to watch me playing in the pen with my pig friends.

"Wow," Bryan said. "It's a baby donkey!"

I decided this new creature might want to play, too! I raced over to the fence to sniff him. He put a furry nose down inside the pen to sniff me back.

I could smell that he was very young. His breath carried the sweet odor of the green grass he had been eating. I sometimes eat grass, too, but only a blade or two at a time. This not-dog, not-horse animal smelled like he never ate anything *but* grass.

I've learned over time that cats and rabbits and weasels and skunks and crows all eat different things, most of it pretty disgust-

ing. They don't know what good dogs know, which is how to sit by a table and wait until toast comes their way—with or without peanut butter. Nothing tastes better than a treat given to me by my girl's hand.

This is something most animals don't seem to care about. If this grass-eating creature was ever lucky enough to be inside the house at dinner time, I bet he would just ignore what was up on the table and hope to be let out to chew on the lawn.

Scamper and Dash charged over to sniff at the new animal's nose through the fence. Maggie Rose came close, too. She reached out and stroked the new animal's muzzle. "I've never seen a baby donkey before. It's so cute!"

A woman I remembered smelling before came over from a house nearby. I wagged in her direction. "That's Burrito," the woman said. "I just picked him up this morning."

She leaned against the fence next to Maggie Rose and Bryan. Mom went over and shook her hand. "Are you Kelly?" Mom asked.

"That'd be me," the woman agreed cheerfully. "You remember me, Maggie Rose? You came with your dad to bring me the little pigs when they were just babies."

I looked at my girl because I'd heard her

name. She nodded. "Is this your donkey?" she asked.

That was the second time my girl had said "donkey." I wondered if the new word had anything to do with this new animal I was sniffing.

"Yes, and he's a sweetie," the woman, Kelly, replied. "Want to give him a treat?"

Treat! Now that's a word that will get a dog's attention. I abandoned Scamper and Dash and squirmed under the fence. The donkey not-dog watched me but didn't change expression or make any noise or wag his tail at all. I did my very best Sit at Maggie Rose's feet to show that I was ready for any treats that might be showing up.

Maggie Rose laughed. "Oh, Lily," she said. "Not for you."

I wagged. *Yes, I am Lily and I am very good and I would like my treat now, please.*

Kelly handed Maggie Rose something. I could smell what it was—a carrot.

I have tried carrots before. They are not too bad, even though you have to chew at them a lot. They come apart in bits, like a squeaky toy. And you can swallow them, just like pieces of a squeaky toy. But they are not treats. So I kept doing Sit, waiting for the real dog treat.

Maggie Rose didn't even seem to notice my good Sit! She held her hand out the way Kelly showed her—flat, with the carrot resting on her palm.

The donkey was very interested in that carrot. He stuck his big nose right into Maggie Rose's hand.

Maggie Rose giggled. "It tickles!" she exclaimed as the donkey crunched up the carrot.

I gave up doing Sit. Nobody was even paying attention, and it wasn't worth doing it for a carrot, anyway. I watched as Bryan held out his peanut-butter-flavored palm with another carrot. That donkey was acting like a carrot was as good as a chicken treat. Donkeys must not be as smart as dogs. Any dog would know that a carrot is not that exciting.

Kelly rubbed the donkey behind the ears. I like getting scratched there, too, so I went up to Maggie Rose and nudged her hand. She had forgotten my treat, but she could give me a scratch at least.

She did.

"I love donkeys," said Kelly. "I had one for years—Mr. Jack. But he died last winter."

"Oh dear, I'm sorry," said Mom.

"That's too bad," Bryan said.

"He had a good long life," Kelly said. "I finally decided I was ready for a new donkey, and I got this one from a farm down the way. I named him Burrito because a *burro* is a small donkey, and he's just a little guy. I figured a little *burro* should be a Burrito! He's kind of shy, but I'm hoping he'll get along with the other animals. The pigs really seem to like him. They were all playing in the big field together this morning. Let's try it again."

She climbed over the fence and opened up a gate to the pigs' pen.

Scamper and Dash squealed with excitement and darted through the gate so fast they nearly knocked Kelly over.

The donkey seemed just as happy. He kicked out his back legs and shook his head and then he ran across the grass, snorting and making more of those loud, funny noises.

Scamper and Dash raced behind him.

Chase-Me! They were doing Chase-Me! I know a lot of games—I can play It's-My-Ball-Not-Yours and Let's-Carry-a-Stick and Dig-in-the-Dirt. But of all games, Chase-Me is the best. I did not want to be left behind, so I ran after Scamper and Dash and the donkey.

"Go, Lily!" Maggie Rose called.

I loved the farm!

The pigs and I ran until we felt like rolling, and then we rolled on the ground in one big pile. The donkey came trotting up to us and flopped down, too, and we all rolled. It was so much fun!

Then I stood up and shook because of another new odor on the air. The farm was full
of them!

I turned and saw two boys, one about my
girl's size and one much bigger. They were
coming up the road, and they were leading a
strange animal by a leash that connected to
a harness around his head.

I had met this animal before.

I heard the new woman, Kelly, say, "Oh, look, here comes Ringo! Doesn't he look handsome!"

The new arrival was a little like a horse, but he had a much longer neck and a smaller head. His fur was fuzzy and looked soft. His head was up so high, it was taller than even the taller of the two boys.

We get a lot of animals coming and going at Work, but this one was one of the strangest-looking. I was about to trot over to greet it and the new boys, but Maggie Rose called me and I went to her side, since that's what good dogs do.

"Is that a llama?" Bryan asked.

"Yep. Name's Ringo. Would you like to pet him? He was over at the neighbor's place, getting his coat groomed," Kelly replied.

"I saw him when I was here before. He didn't want to play with Lily," Maggie Rose added.

Kelly waved her hand. "Let Ringo loose, boys! And come on over."

The taller boy unclipped the horse-thing's leash and it immediately trotted over to where Scamper, Dash, and the donkey were still wrestling in the grass. All three stopped playing to see what this new animal would do.

The horse-thing ignored the pigs. It came right toward the little donkey, stamping with its hard hooves.

"Oh no!" Maggie Rose cried.

She was unhappy. And the little donkey scrambled to his feet and backed away from the big horse-thing. I could tell something was wrong. My new friend was in danger!

I broke out of Sit and raced across the field, coming to a stop directly in front of the horse-thing. I barked, letting it know that if it wanted to hurt the donkey, it would have to deal with a dog.

The horse-thing had large dark eyes with very long eyelashes. He blinked and studied me carefully. Then he made the strangest sound I had ever heard an animal make. His mouth stayed closed, but somehow he brayed a little like the donkey and honked a little like a goose and squeaked kind of like my squeaky toy back Home.

Then he spat right at me. Blinking, I backed away. I'd never been spat at before!

I barked again because I couldn't think of what else to do.

The little donkey was just as confused as I was. He ran around behind me and shook his head. Scamper and Dash seemed nervous and turned and fled back through the gate to their pen.

The two boys came running up. The taller one grabbed the harness on the horse-thing and snicked the leash back onto it. He pulled the spitting, moaning creature back while the younger one came up and put his arms around the donkey.

Soon Maggie Rose and Kelly joined us. Kelly was panting a little.

"Lily!" my girl said. Then she put my leash on, so that now there were two of us on leashes. I hoped she understood I had not been a bad dog. I'd just been trying to help my friend.

The donkey was still being hugged by the smaller boy. He had a scent I recognized. I'd met him before.

"Thank you so much, Kurt, for grabbing Ringo. And you, Bobby, for holding on to poor Burrito," Kelly said.

"Mom and Bryan are putting Scamper and Dash back in their pen," Maggie Rose said.

The horse-thing was eyeing me coldly. Then it turned its head and stared at the donkey. Who would want such a mean thing as a pet? Maybe Kelly should come down to Work and meet some nice animals.

"Hi!" the younger boy exclaimed. "You're

the one who brought the pigs, right? You're Maggie?"

"Maggie Rose. I remember you, Bobby," my girl replied. "Let's put Lily and Burrito into the pen with the pigs. They're all friends."

"Good idea," Kelly said. "And Kurt, you keep hold of Ringo."

The tall boy nodded. "He sure doesn't like that donkey," he said.

We went over to where Scamper and Dash were back behind their fence. Kelly opened a gate and the younger boy led the donkey in. My girl unsnapped my leash. I went under the fence because I could tell that's what she wanted, but I stood near the people while the donkey went to lie down with Sadie and her two big baby pigs.

The humans were talking to each other. Because I am a very smart dog, I figured out that the taller boy was Kurt, and the boy Maggie Rose's age was Bobby.

The spitting, moaning, mean horse-thing was called Ringo. He stood near the people while they talked, and I kept an eye on him while he kept an eye on me. If he spat at Maggie Rose, I would have to bite him right on one of his hooves. I didn't really want to do that, so I hoped he would keep his spit to himself.

"Ringo doesn't like Burrito at all!" Kelly said, shaking her head. "It's so strange. I've never seen him behave that aggressively before toward any of my other animals."

"He didn't like Lily very much, either," Maggie Rose added. I wagged at my name.

"I've heard that llamas can be like that," Mom put in. "They might decide that another animal is a threat for no reason anyone can figure out. Can you keep the two of them separated?"

Kelly put both hands in her pockets. "For right now I can. But Ringo really does have to be free to roam around the whole farm. He's like a guard dog—he keeps an eye on all the animals, and he makes a lot of noise if any predators come near. We're right in the mountains, and there are coyotes around."

"That's what our donkeys do on our ranch," Bobby said. "They keep our place safe from predators."

"Donkeys guard the ranch? What do you mean?" my girl asked.

6

I wagged because my girl had said something, even though I hadn't heard my name.

"No, seriously, they really do act like security guards," Bobby insisted.

"It's funny how they go about it," taller-boy Kurt said. "If the donkeys see anything, like a deer passing by, first their ears all go up and point right at it. Like the way we would point our fingers."

Kurt pointed at me, so I did Sit.

"Then they line up," Bobby said.

"Right," Kurt agreed. "Side by side at the fence, they line up and start up braying. That's to let us know there's something out there."

"What happens if it's a mountain lion? Or a bear?" Bryan wanted to know.

"Then they turn around and show their rear ends!" Kurt hooted.

Nobody told me how good my Sit was, so I got up and stretched.

"And that's scary?" Bryan asked, grinning.

"Yeah, actually, because a kick from a donkey can hurt a mountain lion or even kill it. They could give a bear a hard time," Kurt explained. "It never comes to that, though. We had a mountain lion come up to the ranch once, and when the donkeys lined up it took off for the hills."

"That same cougar came sniffing around here, too, and Ringo chased him off," Kelly agreed. "Nobody wants to be stomped by a llama. It would crush a paw."

"So if Ringo stomps on Burrito, he could really get hurt?" Maggie Rose asked in a small voice.

All the people stopped talking. For some reason, they turned to look at Burrito, who was still sleeping with the pigs. I yawned, thinking a nap might be a good idea.

"I think I should never have bought another

donkey," Kelly murmured sadly. "I don't know what I'm going to do now."

"Know what?" Kurt said suddenly. "I'll bet my dad would want Burrito. He was saying just the other day that all our donkeys are getting to be pretty old. Spud's our oldest, and he's more than thirty."

"Your dad would take Burrito? That would be wonderful," Kelly replied. "That would solve all our problems!"

I noticed that everyone was suddenly more cheerful now. I glanced around but didn't see anything that might explain the change, like a toy.

Kelly went into the pen and hooked a rope around Burrito and led him out through the gate. I wiggled out under the fence and my girl put me on a leash.

I realized that Burrito smelled very much the same as Scamper and Dash. There was a donkey smell underneath, one that was all his own, but on top of that smell there was a lot of pig.

"Well, Burrito, let's go next door and see how you like being with a herd of your own kind," Kelly said.

We all went for a walk! Well, not Ringo, who stayed behind so he could glare and spit at everything. The rest of us headed down a road. I was with my girl, who walked next to Bobby, and Kurt was beside Bryan. Mom and Kelly and Burrito were at the rear.

"We're getting some chickens soon," Bobby told Maggie Rose. "Maybe you could come and get eggs sometime!"

"That would be nice," Maggie Rose agreed shyly.

I smelled where we were going long before we got there. The scent of donkey was very strong on the air. There were also other animals, especially horses. Another farm! I couldn't wait to get back Home so Brewster could smell all the new odors on my fur.

We turned up a rutted driveway and I stopped dead in my tracks, because there in the dirt was the most amazing thing I'd ever sniffed.

Poop! But not just any poop. Giant poop! It was a pile of poop bigger than my head! And not dog poop, either. I have smelled plenty of that. This smelled different, sort of grassy. I sniffed deeply and realized that a horse had left this poop here for me.

"Maggie Rose, don't let Lily roll in that!" Mom called. She was farther back, still walking with Burrito and Kelly.

"I'm trying!" Maggie Rose called. She pulled hard on my leash. "Lily, come on! Lily, I said *come*!"

Of course I knew that I should do what my girl said, but really? Leave the horse poop before I'd smelled it all? I wondered if I should take a little taste. I gave it a lick. Not bad!

"Ugh, Lily, stop it!" said Maggie Rose, and she pulled so hard on my leash that I was forced to leave the poop before I was done sniffing.

At the top of the driveway I could see the donkeys, in a big field next to a building. Burrito made a squealing, braying sound, and I realized that he'd noticed the donkeys, too. One of the donkeys brayed back, and they all lined up at the fence to watch us coming. They had big ears that stood straight up on their heads instead of flopping down like most dogs' do. Those ears swung around to point right at us.

Maggie Rose pulled me close on my leash. "They're pointing their ears. Does that mean they're going to try to kick Lily?"

"No, don't worry," Bobby told Maggie Rose. "The donkeys are used to dogs. We've got

three. I think they're most interested in Burrito, actually. I'm going to go get them some treats that they like, and we'll use those to help them get used to Burrito. It's going to work, I'm sure."

"Where's your father?" Kelly asked.

"He rode off to check on our cattle. Once we get Burrito settled in, I'll grab a horse and go and let him know what's going on," Kurt replied. He looked at Bryan. "You want to come along?"

ryan blinked in surprise. "Oh. Uh, I never rode on a horse before."

"S'okay, I'll put you up on Daisy. She's pretty much the most gentle horse in the world," Kurt replied.

"You should go, Bryan," Maggie Rose said.

Bryan grinned. "Yeah, okay, cool."

Bobby ran toward a house, and the rest of us waited for him to come back. I drank in the smell of the grown-up donkeys that was drifting toward us on the breeze. They were still all watching us, probably amazed at what a good dog I was being.

The door of the house door banged open, and Bobby came charging back out. He had something in his hands that smelled sweet and juicy. Not as sweet and juicy as chicken, though.

"Watermelon!" exclaimed Maggie Rose.

"Donkeys love it," Kurt said. Bobby handed Maggie Rose and Bryan a couple of pieces, but he did not give any to me, even though I was willing to take a bite to see if I liked it.

The grown-up donkeys were very interested in the watermelon. They stretched their necks over the fence and made happy snorting sounds. Maggie Rose and Bryan held out dripping hands and the donkeys gobbled down the slices of wet stuff as if they were treats. I sniffed at some splashes of juice that fell on the dirt at our feet, but didn't lick it.

"Okay!" Kurt said. "Let Burrito in!"

Kelly opened a gate in the fence and led little Burrito into the donkey yard.

The grown-up donkeys all swung around to glare at Burrito. Their ears pointed toward him.

Burrito took a few steps toward the other donkeys. Then he stopped.

I have seen dogs do that, when they want

to play with some new dogs, but they are not sure that the new dogs want to play with them. Burrito was not sure. He was ready to run if he had to.

And he did have to! Two of the donkeys charged right at Burrito, while the other two brayed with their loud, squealing voices. Burrito fled in panic.

"Oh no!" Maggie Rose cried.

I started to dart forward, ready to protect my friend, but my leash stopped me short. Kurt and Bobby ran into the yard, waving their hands. The grown-up donkeys shied away from the boys, while Kelly quickly led Burrito back out to be with us.

"What in the world?" Kelly wondered. "Why did they do that?"

Mom shook her head. "That's not how donkeys normally behave."

I could tell Burrito was sad. His head was low, and he was staring at the other donkeys.

Maggie Rose petted his nose, but it did not seem to cheer him up.

"Poor Burrito," she murmured.

"It's like when you go to a new school and none of the kids like you," Bryan said.

Everyone was quiet for a moment. "I had friends the very first day," Maggie Rose said softly. "You'll make friends, too, Bryan."

Now Bryan seemed as sad as the baby donkey.

Burrito had backed into thick grass. I walked over to him and touched noses with him to help him calm down.

The other donkeys were watching Burrito closely. Every now and then, one stomped in his direction.

This was not fun! I ran in a circle around Burrito to show all the donkeys how we could play if we wanted to. But Burrito did not want to do Chase. He stayed still, watching the other donkeys as closely as they were watching him.

Meanwhile, Maggie Rose was spinning because my leash was wound all around her now. She reached down and unclicked me.

I figured it would not hurt if I went to see the other donkeys, since Burrito wasn't cheering up. I slid in under the fence rail

and trotted up to the grown-up donkeys and
lifted my nose.

"Be careful, Lily!" Maggie Rose warned.

One of the big donkeys put her nose down
so we could sniff. Then the others did the
same thing.

I sniffed all the noses. Then I ran a little

way into the grass and looked back. Did they know what that meant?

They did! One trotted forward. I ran more, and she came after me.

The others seemed to get the idea. They followed, lowering their heads. I ran in a circle, and the donkeys came with me—all but one, a big male. I could smell that he was very old, and maybe (like Brewster) he would rather nap than run. He dropped his head to snatch a mouthful of grass with a dandelion in it.

I looked up and saw the people and Burrito on the other side of the fence. Burrito was watching us run and chase and chew dandelions. But the little donkey was all by himself.

That was sad. I had all these donkeys to play with, and Burrito had nobody. I squirmed back under the fence and ran up to Maggie Rose.

"Good dog, Lily!" she praised.

I love being told "good dog." Next, I hurried over to Burrito.

Burrito put his head down to meet me and sniffed me all over. I thought he probably liked the smell of donkey that was painted on my fur, just as I loved the smell of pig that was painted on his.

"The donkeys are friendly to Lily," Maggie Rose said. "Why don't they like Burrito?"

"I don't know," Mom said, shaking her head. "I really don't know what's going on."

"Lily likes Burrito," Maggie Rose pointed out.

"Poor little Burrito!" Kelly said, stroking Burrito's nose and rubbing him behind his ears. "First Ringo didn't like him, and now these other donkeys don't like him, either. What am I going to do?"

"I guess it's time to go get my dad," Kurt said. He looked at Bryan. "You ready?"

What happened next was something a dog could never understand. Maggie Rose and the boys took me over to another pen, while Kelly and Mom stayed behind with Burrito. I did not slide under the rails of this fence, because there were horses in there.

In my opinion, horses are too big for their own good. A donkey is about the right size to play with, but a horse is gigantic. They have heads that are bigger than some dogs I have known! Why does any animal need a head that big?

And horses don't seem to play much, either. Mostly they just stand and stare, the way Burrito was gazing at the grown-up donkeys. Maybe that means that horses are sad. But if they are, I don't feel sorry for them, because I've never met one who was friendly to a dog. They don't hum and spit, but they're not going to cuddle up with me, either.

I was absolutely astounded when Kurt and Bobby led Bryan over to a horse and, with a heave, helped him climb on the giant beast's back!

I didn't know if I should bark or whine or snarl, so I just watched in amazement. He couldn't be happy up there on such a huge creature's back! But he was grinning down at us.

Then Kurt swung himself up on another

horse. I glanced up at my girl in alarm. Were
we going to get on a horse?

Bobby pulled open a gate and the boys on
their horses stepped through it. I backed
away from those hard hooves.

"It's okay, Lily," Maggie Rose said. I heard
my name and thought she was probably say-

ing she did not understand why her brother and Kurt were sitting on top of horses.

"Takes us about an hour to get out to where my dad's tending to the cattle," Kurt told us.

"We'll be fine," Mom assured him.

"My dad's pretty much an expert on donkeys. He'll figure out what's going on here," Bobby said as the horses turned their big butts toward us and wandered off.

Poor Bryan, stuck up on a horse.

We returned to Mom and Kelly and Burrito. "Maybe your father will have an idea how to introduce Burrito to the other animals that won't cause so much stress," Mom told Bobby.

"Burrito seems really sad," Maggie Rose said. She sat down in the grass with a sigh.

Nobody was very happy. The farm was such a delightful place, with donkeys and big piles of poop. It was too bad there had to be horses around, but I guessed without the

horses, there would not be any horse poop—
and horse poop was pretty amazing. So why
were the humans so quiet? I pushed against
Maggie Rose to soak up the comfort of being
near her.

"Ugh, Lily! You stink!" Maggie Rose said.
"You smell like a donkey!"

I snuggled closer. I knew she was telling
me how much she loved being with me.

Mom leaned down and sniffed. "Actually,
Lily smells like a pig," she said. "Very much
so. Definitely bath time when we get home."

"Oh, Lily, you're going to make me smell
like pig, too." Maggie Rose scratched gently
at the back of my neck.

Then her fingers stopped.

I looked up at her to see why the scratching
was no longer happening.

"Mom," she said. "Mom?"

"What is it, honey?" Mom asked.

"Lily smells like a pig?"

"She really does. Can't you smell it?"

"I sure can," Bobby agreed.

"What if Burrito does, too?" Maggie Rose went on. "He likes to play with the baby pigs. He was playing with them all morning. What if the grown-up donkeys don't like him because he doesn't smell right to them? He's a baby donkey, but he doesn't smell like one!"

Mom blinked. "Maggie Rose, that's an idea!"

"We've got a hose on the side of the house and some shampoo right there," Bobby said. He sounded hopeful.

And then something truly ridiculous happened.

A bath! Maggie Rose gave me a bath!

Sometimes she does this at home, and I do not appreciate it. I only let her because I love her so much. Usually she does it in the tub, and I have to run around the house afterward and roll on all the rugs and carpets until my fur smells right again.

But this time there wasn't even a tub. She tied my leash to a fence and got me wet with water from a hose and rubbed soap into my fur. I wiggled and squirmed and tried to let her know that this was obviously playtime, not bath time.

It looked like Burrito was getting the same treatment. Mom and Kelly held him while Bobby worked soap and water into his skin.

Poor Burrito. First the spitting, moaning horse-creature was angry with him, and then he didn't get to play with the other donkeys, and now a bath! If I could be in charge of farms, there would be no spitting and no moaning and no horses (but still horse poop, of course) and no baths. But dogs don't get to make decisions about things like that, which is very sad.

"Stop wiggling, Lily. You have to get clean!"

Maggie Rose told me, rubbing soap along my back. "No, stop it! No!"

I wish I knew why humans are so fond of that word "No." I have never met a person who didn't say "No!" at one time or another. It never makes anything better.

Finally, Maggie Rose squirted clean water over me, and I shook and shook until the tags on my collar rang. I looked around for a rug to roll on, but I did not see one. Maggie Rose untied my leash from the fencepost.

It looked like Burrito's bath was over, too. His fur was damp, and he seemed even gloomier than before.

"Well, that's as clean as we're going to get this little guy, I guess," Kelly said.

"Lily's all clean, too!"
Maggie Rose beamed. I

gave her a sour look. Why was she so happy? Didn't she realize that I'd just had a bath and it had been dreadful?

"So," Mom said, "let's take Burrito back and see if he's any more welcome, now that he no longer smells like a pig!"

Things were looking
better. Maggie Rose
led me, and Bobby led Burrito, away from the
bath area and toward a marvelously fragrant
pile of horse poop, so fresh it was buzzing
with flies. A quick roll in that, I knew, would
get this awful soapy stink off of my fur. And
when I was done, Burrito would probably
want to take a turn.

"No, Lily!"

That word again, accompanied by a swift

tug on my leash. I didn't even get to put my nose to the dark lumps in the dirt before I was dragged away.

Even though I love my girl, she just doesn't understand some things. Like horse poop.

Soon we were all back at the fence with the older donkeys milling around on the other side. Their ears came up at our approach. Everybody on our side seemed excited and a little nervous. I couldn't tell what the donkeys were feeling, though.

"Okay, let's give it another try," Mom said. She led Burrito on his leash toward the fence. "I hope this works!"

Mom opened the gate and Burrito stepped hesitantly into the donkey yard. He still seemed pretty glum. I thought I knew the reason why—the other donkeys hadn't liked Burrito earlier. And if they didn't like him, they wouldn't play with him. And nothing is fun when there's no playing.

Why was Mom trying this again? Why didn't we all go back to the pigs and wrestle in the mud? Then Burrito and I could both get rid of the bath smells and have some fun with animals that actually *liked* baby donkeys.

Maggie Rose bent down and unsnapped my leash. "Go and help, Lily," she whispered to me.

Since Burrito was still on Mom's leash and couldn't play, I decided to join the grown-up donkeys. They might not like a Burrito very much, but they liked a Lily! I crawled under the fence and dashed up to my donkey friends, ready for fun.

But they did not seem very interested in me. They had all turned to look right at Burrito and Mom. Their ears swiveled toward the littler donkey. The oldest one stomped and let out a challenging bray.

Burrito backed up a few steps. He looked sad and also nervous.

This was silly. I liked to run. The donkeys liked to run. Burrito liked to run. Why didn't we all do some running right now? Why stomp and stare? I jumped and bowed and wagged so that the donkeys would get the message that there was a dog in their yard who was ready for some serious playing.

The donkeys ignored me. The oldest one brayed again, more loudly. He glared at Burrito.

"That's Spud," Bobby called. "He's the most grumpy of them all."

"I don't think this is working," Kelly added. She sounded worried.

Mom shook her head and pulled on Burrito's leash. She led the little donkey back through the gate. "I'm so sorry, Maggie Rose. It was a good idea. I'm surprised that it didn't work."

"Oh, poor Burrito!" Maggie Rose said. She hugged the little donkey's neck.

The bigger donkeys in the field with me seemed to relax once Burrito was on the other side of the fence. I ran in a little circle and back to them. Did they get the hint? Were they ready to do Chase-Me?

It was hard to tell. I ran in a bigger circle so they would definitely be able to see what I wanted.

Two donkeys settled down, grabbing mouthfuls of grass and munching it. But the other two, who seemed younger, lowered their heads and trotted after me. Then, once they got the idea of running into their heads, they decided they liked it! They took off at a gallop,

dashing all the way around the field. They were fast! I could not keep up, although I tried my best.

After a big circle around the fence, we came back to where we had started. I was panting. The two Chase-Me donkeys both sniffed at me, and the big old donkey huffed out a long breath before he went back to munching.

"Spud's not so angry now," Bobby observed.

I glanced over to see Maggie Rose still hugging Burrito. I didn't mind other animals getting affection, as long as they knew Maggie Rose was *my* girl. But I thought she would have more fun if she were with me in the donkey yard. And Burrito was a donkey. He should come and play with the other donkeys.

This farm was wonderful, but it had some very strange rules. Baths for no reason. People stuck up on horses. Nobody allowed to roll in horse poop, which is obviously what it is for. Baby donkeys not allowed to play with grown-up donkeys.

But people make rules and dogs follow them. That's how it has always been, even though the rules might not always make sense.

I wiggled back under the fence and trotted up to Maggie Rose. I sniffed at her shoes and licked her knee.

"Oh, Silly Lily," she said. She reached down to pat me.

Burrito lowered his nose to touch mine. I bowed low and wiggled my rump up high. Then I ran in a circle again.

"Mom, let go of his rope. I think Burrito wants to play with Lily!"

Burrito did Chase-Me! We didn't get very far, though, before he came to a halt and gazed at me with his big, mournful eyes. But at least he'd tried. He followed me back to my girl, who petted him. Bobby petted him, too.

"Look, Mom!" Maggie Rose said softly. "All the donkeys are watching Lily and Burrito play!"

"They're certainly interested," Mom agreed.

"They're not pointing their ears at us," Bobby said. "See? So they're just watching now."

Kelly put a hand out and stroked Burrito. "Do you think that means they might be getting used to this little guy?"

Burrito was certainly getting a lot of attention from people, but being petted didn't seem to cheer him up the way it would a dog.

"They're seeing that Lily is friends with Burrito," Maggie Rose said. "And they're friends with Lily. So maybe they'll get the idea that Burrito should be their friend, too."

"Maybe," Mom replied thoughtfully.

Maggie Rose shook her head. "No, Mom, it's true. You know how all the animals at the rescue like Lily so much? I bet those big donkeys do, too. And they're thinking that if they like Lily, and Lily likes Burrito, then maybe the baby donkey is okay."

Bobby grinned. "That could be right! Whenever we get a new horse, we put it on one side of the fence and leave the rest of the herd corralled on the other side. That way, they get used to each other with a fence between them. And then my Dad will give apples to the old horses, and an apple to the new one. He'll go back and forth, handing out apples and carrots, and then when he opens the corral, the new horse is accepted as part of the family!"

"Lily! Go back inside with the donkeys!" Maggie Rose urged.

She obviously wanted me to do something, so I did Sit. That didn't seem to be the right thing, though. Maggie Rose went to the fence, patted her legs, and pointed to the place where I'd been crawling under the rails. "Go, Lily!"

I hesitated. "Go" sounded a little like "no." But there was no horse poop around for her to get all worked up again. So maybe she was saying something else. . . .

Maggie Rose pointed under the fence again. I went over to her and sniffed where she was pointing. There was nothing there but the faint smell of me, where I'd crawled under the fence before.

"Play with the donkeys, Lily!"

I didn't know what Maggie Rose wanted, so I decided it was best to do something fun—like play with the donkeys. I wiggled back into their yard and trotted up to the oldest one, doing a play bow. He eyed me suspiciously.

"Go on, Spud! Play with the dog!" Bobby said.

I spun in a circle. The donkey watched. I

bowed again. No reaction. I kicked up grass as I did a short dash around him, and then he and the other old one chased me a short way. They stopped after a few steps, just like Burrito.

Now it was time for me to chase them back! But the two older donkeys were more interested in eating grass. The two younger ones got the idea, though, and they trotted ahead of me a little, while I ran behind their tails.

"Good dog, Lily!" Maggie Rose called.

There are times when "good dog" leads to treats, so I trotted straight to my girl's side. The donkeys followed me as far as the fence.

No treat from my girl, but sometimes being called "good dog" is reward enough.

"Donkeys are watching," Bobby told us.

The bigger donkeys were all gathered at the fence now. Mom picked up Burrito's leash. "Back up, Maggie Rose," Mom said softly. "I don't want you near in case anybody starts kicking."

My girl backed away several steps. She stood very still. Mom led Burrito right up to the fence.

A grasshopper jumped

out of the dirt at my feet, so I chased it and tried to pounce on it with both front paws. It whirred away, and I jumped again, but I didn't catch it. Where had it gone?

I looked around for the grasshopper and noticed what was happening at the fence.

The older donkeys were sniffing Burrito! They had their long necks stretched over the fence and their soft noses were nuzzling at Burrito's face.

Nobody brayed. Nobody stared. Nobody stomped.

Burrito seemed to get a little braver and moved closer. The other donkeys could now sniff all along his neck and back.

Sniffing is the best way to make friends, of course. I've often wondered why people don't sniff each other when they meet. It's one of the many strange things about people. I've seen people shake Bryan's hand up and down, but nobody has ever thought to

grab his fingers and smell them and maybe lick the traces of peanut butter from his skin.

Certainly *I've* licked him. Even when there's no actual peanut butter clinging to his hands, it's a nice thing to do.

Maggie Rose was bouncing up and down

on her toes the way she does when she's really excited. "It's working! It's working!" she said. "They're figuring out that he smells like a donkey now! They like him!"

"I think you're right!" Mom said. She gently tugged on Burrito's leash and led him over to the gate and into the donkey yard. "Come with me, Lily! Come!"

We were all going to get to play together at last?

I dashed through the open gate and up to Mom, who still held Burrito's leash. The other donkeys slowly approached. A few put their big heads down where I could reach them, and there was more sniffing. It must have been nice for the donkeys, being sniffed by a dog.

I was proud to have taught the donkeys how to play Chase-Me and how to greet a stranger by sniffing. They'd learned very well. If I could get Maggie Rose to hand them some chicken treats, they'd probably give up eating grass forever.

The oldest donkey let out a long sigh that made his nostrils flap.

He stretched out his neck and rested his chin on Burrito's back.

Soon all the donkeys were pressed together, sort of like when I take a nap curled up with Brewster and Maggie Rose. Except we always lie down to nap, and the donkeys were still standing up.

"They do that when they're really happy," Bobby said.

Mom and I left the donkey yard, and I went to Maggie Rose.

"What a smart dog you have," Kelly told her.

Eventually the grown-up donkeys wandered off, staying in pairs as they bit at the grass. Soon they were far out in the field. Every one of them.

Except Burrito.

Burrito stood without moving, watching the other donkeys. He put his head down to nose at the grass, but he didn't take a bite.

"Burrito's still sad!" Maggie Rose exclaimed.

"Why doesn't he go out into the field with the other donkeys?" Kelly asked.

"He does seem sad. I have no idea why," Mom agreed.

Burrito was standing and staring at

nothing. He seemed really glum. I wondered if anyone had a squeaky toy we could use to liven things up.

"Here comes Dad," Bobby said.

Dad? I knew who Dad was. I looked around, but I could not smell or see Dad. What I did see, though, were three of those ridiculously large horses trotting toward us. Kurt was still stuck on top of one and poor

Bryan was on another, and there was a man with them, and he was stuck, too.

There were three dogs, their tongues all lolling out, running alongside this strange parade. They stopped when the horses did, and then the man figured out how to get off the horse's back. I was very ready to make friends with the dogs, but they followed Kurt and Bryan and the third horse, who all went around the barn and disappeared.

"Afternoon," the man called with a grin as he approached. "How are you, Kelly?"

"Hi, Matthew. This is my friend from the animal rescue, Chelsea, and her daughter, Maggie Rose."

"And the dog is Lily," Bobby added. "Hi, Dad."

I glanced up at Bobby. He'd said "Dad" again. He sure was confused—Dad wasn't here!

"Glad to meet all of you. Your son Bryan is

a good worker, ma'am," the man told Mom. "Helped me move my herd to fresh pasture."

"Bryan?" Mom repeated, surprised. "He's never ridden a horse before."

"Well, he's a natural," the man replied. He smiled at Burrito, who was still standing by himself. "And look at this beauty! Kurt told me your problem with the llama, Kelly. I could have saved you some trouble—donkeys and llamas don't usually get along unless they're raised up together."

"I just wanted him because he was so cute," Kelly replied with a shake of her head.

"Well, I've been thinking I need to get a few young ones. Old Spud's getting on in his years," the man answered. "Be happy to give you what you paid for him."

Bryan came running up, panting and looking excited. "I had so much fun!" he said, grinning. He certainly was happier than he'd been this morning.

The man grinned. "If hard work is your idea of fun, young man, I'd like to have you visit more often."

Bryan nodded. "Kurt said to tell you he's tending to the horses and then he'll feed the dogs their dinner."

I raised my head sharply. *Dogs? Dinner?*

"But Burrito's sad!" Maggie Rose said impatiently.

The man blinked at her. "Sad, you say?"

"Look at him. Even Lily can't cheer him up."

I wagged at my name. If we were talking about dogs and dinner and Lily then things were definitely looking good.

The man and Mom went through the gate and up to Burrito, who didn't wag or lick or greet them in any way.

The man ran his hands up and down the donkey's back and front legs. "Don't see anything wrong, here."

"I'm a veterinarian," Mom said with a nod. "I think he's perfectly healthy. But he does seem depressed."

The man and Mom came back to our side of the fence. I smelled their hands. His carried the odor of horses, some other animals I couldn't identify, and Burrito the donkey. "You just pick him up this morning?" he asked Kelly.

"Yes, and he seemed fine to me then. Very lively when I first saw him," Kelly replied.

The man took off his big hat for a moment, scratching his head. "Then I got nothin'. Usually there's some trouble introducing a new donkey, but if that were the issue, Spud and the others would be right here letting us know it, instead of off in the pasture."

"Maybe he misses his friends," Bryan blurted.

Everyone looked at Bryan, so I did, too.

"It's like when you move to a new place.

You go to school with the other kids, but you miss your old friends," Bryan went on.

Mom reached out and patted Bryan's shoulder gently.

The man raised his eyebrows. "Well, now, maybe you really are a born rancher. Everybody look out there at my donkeys. See anything?"

"They're just eating like always," Bobby replied.

I yawned and scratched my ear with my rear paw.

"I don't know what I'm supposed to see," Mom confessed.

"They're in pairs!" Maggie Rose exclaimed. "See? There's two close together on one side and two close together on the other."

I wagged because Maggie Rose seemed excited.

"That's exactly right, young lady," the man told her with a nod. "Donkeys form what we

call bonded pairs. Not necessarily with a mate, and not always with a brother or a sister, but once they've bonded they do everything together."

"When I met Burrito, he was standing with another one his age!" Kelly exclaimed.

"There you have it," the man replied with a grin.

"Burrito misses his best friend," Bryan said, nodding.

"Well . . . looks like I'm going to need to go get myself another little donkey," the man observed cheerfully. "Let's load Burrito into the trailer so he can pick out the right one for us." He looked at Bryan. "If it's okay with your mother, you can come along, too. I could use a hand."

Bryan looked at Mom, who smiled. "That's fine with me!" she said.

Soon I watched in utter bafflement as they led Burrito to a big car that was attached to another big car. When it trundled away, I was left with Bobby and my girl and Mom and Kelly. Bryan had gone with the man and Burrito.

Where were they taking the little donkey? And why did he get his own car?

aggie Rose put my leash back on and we all went for *another* walk to smell the horse poop. What an amazing day!

Bobby remained behind. Maybe he was going to give the other donkeys their baths now. But Kelly walked with us.

We were soon back at the farm where Scamper and Dash lived. I ignored the ugly horse-thing, who glared at me but didn't spit or moan. Mom and Maggie Rose talked with

Kelly for a long time, and they all said "Lily" a lot, which made me sure they were talking about what a good dog I was and how I should be given some treats immediately.

I wiggled into the pen with Scamper and Dash. They were dozing in a heap with their mother, but they were very happy to wake up for a game of Chase-Me that led us through lots of mud puddles. The mud slipped and slid beneath my paws in a wonderful way, and once I flopped down and skidded on my belly right up to the nose of the mother pig.

Sadie opened her eyes and grunted at me, and I licked her nose and ran off to dig in a corner with Scamper and turned up two apple cores. Scamper ate one and I chewed a little on the other until Dash came and took it away, so of course we had to do Chase some more.

While the three of us were busy, the people stood and talked as people do. "Well, I've got to get back to my chores," Kelly told them.

"Thank you for everything, Chelsea. You, too, Maggie Rose."

"And Lily!" my girl said. I glanced at her but then went back to rolling with pigs.

Eventually Maggie Rose called me and put a leash on me and I was taken on yet *another* walk! Truly this was the most astounding day of my life!

I noticed the horse poop as we passed it again, but I wasn't as excited about it this time.

"You were right to suggest we bring Bryan with us," Mom told Maggie Rose as we walked. "He's really having a good time on the ranch."

"And he figured out what was wrong with Burrito!" Maggie Rose reminded her mother.

"Yes, he did. Maggie Rose, you know that there's not anything we can do about his friend Carter moving away. That's how life is sometimes."

Maggie Rose nodded. "I know. It's like

with the rescue, when we get in a kitten and we all love it, but then we find a home for it and it goes away."

"Exactly. Smart girl."

I saw a grasshopper. I didn't know if it was the same one, but I pounced anyway and then it was *gone*. How do they do that?

Soon we were back up at the donkey yard. The old donkeys were still out searching in the grass for something good to eat, but Burrito was close to the fence, prancing and playing with another baby donkey! I wagged excitedly. A new friend!

The man and Bryan were watching the two little donkeys play. The man turned and smiled as we approached. "Welcome back, you two. I'd like you to meet the newest addition to the family. The lighter-colored one is named Taco."

"Burrito and Taco!" Maggie Rose exclaimed happily.

The leash came off with a *snick* and I wriggled excitedly under the fence and ran up to greet the new donkey, who lowered his nose and sniffed. I knew that I must smell of pig a lot, which was a relief. It was much better than smelling of bath.

We played Chase-Me, which seemed pretty much the only game the donkeys knew. I decided that the next time I came, I would bring a ball.

"Lily!" Maggie Rose called. I went to her, wagging. She snicked the leash onto my collar.

"I mean it, Chelsea. I could use all the help I can get, and your son here is a natural on a horse and a good worker to boot," the man was saying. "Plus, my daughter has piano lessons every Saturday morning right down in town. My wife could bring Bryan back with her, and he could spend the day here on the ranch helping out."

"Would something like that interest you, Bryan?" Mom asked.

Bryan's eyes were as wide as his smile. "Yes!"

Everyone seemed so happy, I just had to wag.

"Here she comes now, in fact," the man observed.

I looked up because a car had stopped in

the driveway. The doors opened. A woman carrying a paper bag waved and went into the house, and a girl ran over to us. She had long hair like Maggie Rose, but she was a little older, I thought. She came right to me and petted me, so I liked her immediately. Her pants smelled like peanut butter, and so did her hands.

"Audrey, meet Maggie Rose, and Mrs. Murphy, and Lily. Oh, and this is Bryan."

"Hi," the girl said. "What grade are you in?"

"Fifth grade," Bryan answered.

"I'm in third," Maggie Rose put in.

"I'm in fifth, too," the girl said.

"Bryan's going to come help out every Saturday for a few hours," the man said mildly. "Maybe you could show him the ropes, Audrey."

The girl, Audrey, nodded. "I'd like that," she said simply.

"That's wonderful," said Mom. "Well, we've really got to head home. Maggie Rose, if you don't mind . . ."

"You know what that means, Lily, you piggy-smelling dog," Maggie Rose told me.

I wagged happily up at her. I was sure that whatever was going to happen next, I would really enjoy it. I felt that way as Maggie Rose took my leash. I felt that way as she led me to

the side of the house. I even felt that way
when she tied my leash to the fence.

But when she turned on the hose, I no longer felt that way.

Baths are the *worst*.

Male donkeys are known as jacks, and female donkeys are jennets or jennies.

In the wild, donkeys live in herds, usually with one male and several females.

Tame donkeys are used to carry loads or to provide milk. Sometimes they also protect other animals on a farm or ranch. They will fight off anything they see as a threat by stomping or kicking.

In the United States, wild donkeys are known as *burros*.

Tame donkeys, like Burrito, usually weigh

between four hundred and five hundred pounds when they are full grown. The largest breed of donkey, called the American Mammoth Jack, can weigh twice as much—between nine hundred and twelve hundred pounds.

Young donkeys are called foals.

If a male donkey and a female horse have a foal, it is called a mule. If a female donkey and a male horse have a foal, it is called a hinny.

If a donkey and a zebra have a foal, it is called a zonkey.

The "hee-haw" sound that donkeys make is called a bray. Donkeys breathe in on the "hee" and out on the "haw."

Donkeys can be territorial, which means they will drive other animals away from a space they think of as theirs. On a farm, a donkey may drive smaller animals like goats, sheep, dogs, or cats out of its pasture.

Ute Ville

W. BRUCE CAMERON is the #1 *New York Times*
bestselling author of *A Dog's Purpose, A Dog's
Journey, A Dog's Way Home, A Dog's Promise,* the
Puppy Tales books for young readers, and the
Lily to the Rescue chapter books. He lives in
California.

WBruceCameronKidsBooks.com

Don't miss these

LILY TO THE RESCUE

adventures from bestselling author

W. BRUCE CAMERON

Go to WBruceCameronKidsBooks.com
for downloadable activities.

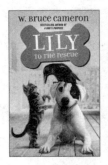
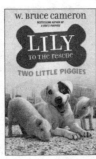
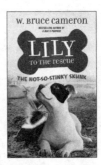

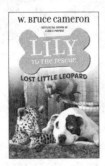
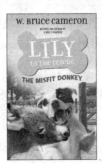
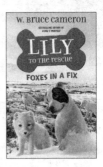